Everything is Peaches

Peaches Monroe's Diary

BOOK #3 of 4

ANGIE PEPPER

Chapter 1

Tuesday, June 28th (The night of the fundraiser)

After the door of the car opened, Dalton's butler stepped out and said, "I'm glad you're here, Ms. Monroe. You can help him in a way I can't." Bernard indicated that I should climb into the back seat with Dalton.

"Hang on a minute," I said to the middle-aged man. "What sort of help are we talking about here?"

There was a hint of a smile under Bernard's thick mustache and a trace of mirth in his English-accented voice. "I'm sure you'll think of something, ma'am."

"I have a boyfriend," I said. "I can't help him in a girlfriend capacity. In fact, I shouldn't even be here."

"And yet, here you are," he said dryly.

I was trying to think of another excuse when Bernard pulled out some of his ninja moves. He put his hand on top of my head and all but shoved me into the back seat. The door closed behind me, and I was in the dark with Dalton.

The front door opened, and Bernard slid into the driver's seat. The privacy glass went up between us. The vehicle began moving.

Dalton hadn't spoken, so I broke the silence. "Who knew that such a fun evening would end with a kidnapping?"

There was no response.

My eyes adjusted to the dark. Dalton was huddled up in the fetal position on the far end of the back seat, watching me warily.

I waved my hand in front of his face. "Hello? Are you totally checked out, or what?"

He blinked and started to stir. "Peaches?" His voice was croaky and uncertain.

"It's me," I said. "Is there another curvy blonde that your butler kidnaps for you? Wait. Don't answer that. I don't want to know."

"Just you," he croaked.

"This is a fine mess you've gotten us into," I said. "I knew you didn't do well under pressure, but you really lost it when that woman threw her drink in your face, didn't you?"

He began to stretch out of the hunched position. "It was just a panic attack. I'm not dying. I'm not having a heart attack." He shuddered then repeated himself. "Just a panic attack. I'm not dying."

"You don't sound very convincing."

"I don't," he agreed.

"If this is what you were paying the folks at that fancy horse ranch in Malibu to get treatment for, you need to get your money back."

He let out a croaky chuckle. "It's not the sort of thing they offer refunds on."

"Well, they should. What did you pay for your last stay?"

He finished straightening out so he was sitting on the seat normally, although a bit stiff in the neck. He named a dollar amount that exceeded the generous advance I'd gotten for my recent underwear modeling gig.

I let out the appropriate stream of swear words to let him know he'd been ripped off. Then I said, "For that much dough, we could buy you a couple of horses and some land to ride them on anytime you want."

He let out another chuckle that was less croaky. "We did more than ride horses at the treatment center."

"Did you talk about your feelings?"

He was slow to answer. "Yes."

"That's the sort of thing you can get for free, from your friends, your family, and even the staff at your friendly neighborhood donut shop."

"I don't have a lot of those things in my life."

"Dalton, if you don't have those things in your life, then that's on you. You're young, rich, and good looking. You should have everything. You should be beating people away with a stick."

He snorted. "Why are you here? To kick me when I'm down?"

"No."

He said, "Really, why *are* you here? The studio only required that we have dinner and be photographed together. You could have gone home."

"I was worried about you." I left out the part where his butler kidnapped me.

"Why?" He sounded much younger than he was, like a little boy.

"I guess... because we're friends."

"We're friends?"

"Sure," I said.

He grinned. Suddenly, he did not look like a person who'd been talking himself out of death by panic attack two minutes earlier.

"Dalton, were you faking that panic attack to get me in the car with you?"

"No." The grin fell off his face. "Is that what you think I am? A manipulative phony?"

"You *are* an actor," I said.

"Only when the cameras are rolling."

"Or when you're researching a role," I said. He started to object, but I held up a finger to stop him. "Don't even try to wriggle your way out of that one. You admitted to me that you were being David, not Dalton, when we first met. That's why you used all his corny lines on me."

The back of the car was quiet for a moment, the only sound being the street noise and the tires on the pavement.

Finally, Dalton said, "I made one mistake, Peaches. One mistake. We can't ever be friends until you can forgive me."

"I suppose I could forgive you, but I can't forget."

"Would you ever forgive me, though? Can you?"

I bit my lower lip. "I suppose I can try. It was just one mistake, after all. We've all made mistakes."

"Thanks. Friend."

He rubbed his upper arms and held himself.

I asked, "Are you cold?" It was a warm summer evening, and it wasn't exactly chilly in the back of the car.

"I feel cold," he said. "The panic attack messes up my thermostat."

"You probably want me to snuggle up against you to warm you up."

"I wasn't going to ask," he said.

I looked out the window. "Where are we going, anyway?"

"Nowhere," he said. "When I get like this, Bentley drives me around until I get sleepy. The forward motion of the vehicle relaxes me. There's some neurological reason, or maybe it's just superstition."

"My parents used to drive Elliot around at night when he was a baby."

Dalton looked hurt. "I'm not a baby. A lot of people in my situation abuse drugs and alcohol to cope with their emotions. They numb themselves to the pressures of being in the public eye. My counselor says it's actually—" He stopped talking, frowned, and turned toward the window. "Never mind."

I felt bad for hurting his feelings. Nisha had been right about Dalton. He was sensitive, underneath his thick armor of charm.

I slid along the leather seat toward him. I gently repositioned one of his arms around me as I snuggled in next to him. I leaned my head on his chest. If Nisha had been cold from a panic attack, I'd have gotten that close to her. It was what friends could do, or so I told myself that night in the car.

Dalton's breathing slowed, and the muscle tension in his body relaxed. It felt, to me, like all the tight elastic threads holding him together were melting away one by one.

"I'm weak," he said. "Like a baby."

Softly, I said, "You're not. I'm sorry I compared you to a baby. Your counselor is right about your coping strategies. Going for a drive is much better than the things some people do, famous or otherwise."

"I'm sorry I got offended. I know you didn't mean anything by it. Plus I like hearing stuff about your family. They're good people."

"I got lucky."

"You sure did."

We were both quiet.

I felt his hot breath on the top of my head, then I heard him sniff.

"Dalton, did you just smell my hair?"

"Yes," he said.

"Friends don't smell each other's hair."

"Duly noted." He squeezed me tighter against him. "What about this? The cuddling?"

"This is a medical necessity," I said. "It's like what we were talking about with Nisha before dinner and everything. I'm your therapy cat. As soon as I put my head on your chest, you relaxed. I'm like a fast-acting drug with no side effects."

"I wouldn't say there are no side effects."

"Shh," I said. "Be quiet and receive your Peaches therapy."

We drove in silence for a few minutes, then he said, "I wonder what that was all about? I've had a drink thrown in my face plenty of times in my acting career, but never in real life."

"You don't know the latest gossip? Bernard didn't look it up and tell you?"

"He was pretty busy keeping me breathing into a paper bag so I didn't pass out."

"You're going to laugh when you hear what it was," I said.

"Try me."

I pulled my head off his chest and told him the whole story—as much as we knew at that time, and as Nisha had relayed it to me.

He didn't laugh.

"This could stick to me forever," he said with a groan.

"But it isn't true. That idiot Jocko Ranger got his dates messed up. Once he finds out I'm only twenty-two, he'll eat his words. Plus look at me." I pulled farther away and looked him in the eyes. "Do I look like a Ranger kid?"

"No," he said. "Lucky you."

"I wonder how many of you are out there."

"How many of *me*?"

"There's only one Dalton Deangelo, of course, but your father bragged about seducing women in twenty minutes flat. I'm sure he didn't stop at two of them outside of marriage."

Dalton frowned. "This could go on for years."

"You could try getting ahead of it. There are those DNA companies that get you in touch with other relatives, if they opt in as well. All you have to do is spit into a vial and send it off. It's not even that expensive. I know someone who just sent in his saliva."

"Who?"

"Nobody you'd know," I said, which wasn't true. I was referring to Garnet Langtree, the teenager who worked for me at the bookstore. His mother was Jade, a singer that Dalton had dated the previous summer. Garnet had gotten the crazy idea Dalton might be his father—they both had similar hair and eyes—until he worked out that Dalton would have barely been a preteen when Garnet had been born. Garnet's famous mother liked younger guys, but not *that* young.

"I've thought about it," Dalton said. "Do you think I should go for it? Send them my saliva? What about my anonymity?"

"They'll have your DNA on file, but your other information is as private as you want it to be," I said. "Assuming they don't get hacked or sell your information. I guess the question is, how much is the information worth to you? Is it worth the risk?"

"You make a good point about getting out ahead of it." Dalton rubbed his chin. "I could have hundreds of half-siblings out there. Can you imagine?"

"It's pretty crazy. But I don't need a test to tell you I'm not one of them, despite certain crazy internet rumors."

"And that's a good thing." He looked out the window and ran his hand through his glossy black hair. "You'll be able to distance yourself from this. I'll be associated with Jocko Ranger forever. Every time he does something tasteless, which I'm sure he won't stop doing, there'll be extra heat on me. The press loves to run those like-father-like-son stories."

"Oh, boo hoo," I said.

He gave me a surprised look. "What?"

"Boo hoo," I repeated. "Your biological father's a big-mouthed, fame-seeking attention sponge, but he's not exactly a serial killer."

Dalton frowned.

"Look on the bright side," I said. "Thanks to his antics, you just got even more famous. Your stock's going up even as we drive around in this car. After your TV show wraps up, you could have an epic movie career. You could be bigger than Jocko Ranger."

He blinked three times. "You do have a real knack for putting things into perspective, Ms. Peaches Monroe."

"I'm glad I could be here for you." I started sliding back to the other side of the seat. "You're not still cold, are you?"

"A little cold," he said. "Come back here for a few more minutes." He adjusted the seat so that it reclined, and shifted over to make room for me.

I slid in, fitting in against him perfectly. I rested my head on his chest once more. He smelled my hair again, breathing in deeply.

He wrapped both of his arms around me.

Bernard continued driving us around the city like a couple of colicky babies.

We fell asleep like that, in each other's arms—or at least I did.

When I woke up about an hour later, we were somewhere quiet, and the car wasn't moving.

Groggily, I asked, "Where are we?"

Dalton said, "We're home, sleepyhead."

I pulled away from him, sat upright, and looked out the car window. We were parked next to a glowing silver tube. We had reached the Airstream trailer that Dalton rented when he was in the city. I hadn't been there since the night he made me dinner and kept me from eating it.

The Airstream was a trap!

My guard went up instantly. Coolly, I said, "You may be home, but I'm not."

He took my hand. "It can be your home tonight. You can stay over and keep me company."

"There's only one bed in there."

"I think the dining area folds into a spare bed," he said. "I'll take that one."

I shook my head. "We talked about this," I said. "We're just friends. I have a boyfriend, and he's not you." I rapped on the glass separating us from the driver.

The privacy window rolled down.

"Bernard, I need a ride to my house," I said. "I can't stay here."

Bernard replied, "Of course. My apologies, ma'am."

"I'll go with you," Dalton said. "I'll keep you company. I'm not ready to hit the hay yet. It's not even that late."

I pointed to the window, to something outside the car. "What's that?"

Dalton turned and looked in the direction I pointed. "What?"

"It's a baby animal in distress," I said. "It needs our help, Dalton. This is exactly what they talked about at the fundraiser tonight."

"Really?" He opened the door and stepped out into the darkness. "I don't see anything."

I grabbed the door, slammed it shut, and told Bernard, "Drive."

Bernard did, with a chuckle.

After we'd rolled past the gates for the estate, I said, "I hate long, uncomfortable goodbyes."

"Don't we all," the driver replied.

Chapter 2

In the days following the fundraiser, Dalton contacted me a few times to thank me for my help. I spoke with him by phone only and politely declined his requests for in-person chats. I had a boyfriend, and it wouldn't be appropriate.

As for the scandal, it blew over quickly, thanks to some other celebrities doing dumb things and taking the heat.

The person who really helped the most, ironically, was Josie Ranger. Dalton's half-sister and Jocko's legitimate offspring tried to leverage some media attention onto herself. She failed. Nothing killed gossip quite like a fame-hungry, B-list celebrity trying to make it a bigger deal, with herself at the heart of everything.

The blowback on my family was minimal. All my aunts, uncles, and cousins had already been scandalized by the pictures of me running through the woods in my underwear. This new story, that was too preposterous to be true, simply capped off the whole Peaches-and-the-actor thing with a funny twist.

To my mother's disappointment, none of her friends believed she'd had an affair with Jocko Ranger all those years ago. The poor thing. She kept her chin up, but I could tell she was devastated. She'd tried insisting to a few close friends that the brief affair with her favorite action hero really *had* happened, but nobody bought it, which was probably for the best.

As for me, my life got back to normal. I had a job to do, and I was busier than ever with the whole move. After many years in its original location, Bookworm Books was moving to a different space on Baker Street in order to cut expenses and survive. The owner, Gordon Olivier, owned several commercial properties in the area, so he was able to shuffle things around in a way most bookstore owners couldn't. I hadn't been thrilled about moving to a smaller location—even though it did have a nice high ceiling—but it was better than having to shut down.

My boyfriend, Adrian Stromquist, had been hired as our operations manager, so he was technically my boss. That made everything we'd been doing for the past few weeks feel taboo, the way it had felt back in high school. I couldn't say the tension of having him try to boss me around wasn't a bit of an aphrodisiac.

That first Saturday in July, I was feeling happy and buoyant as I walked to work. I had a long day ahead of me, but we were closed, so I wouldn't be dealing with any customers. I loved our customers, but it was nice to have a break. Adrian and I would be taking off the fourth to have a big barbecue at my house with both of our families. It promised to be a great weekend.

Adrian was already at work inside the new location when I walked in the back door. He was scowling at our ancient computer monitor and didn't even say hello.

I came over to the counter, picked up his takeout cup, determined it was empty, and proceeded toward the front door.

He growled at my back, "Where do you think you're going?"

"Out to get you another coffee," I said. "That first one you had didn't do the trick."

"I could use some help," he said, not quite growling but still grumpy.

I paused, my hand on the door. "And you'll get it, but not while your face looks like that."

"What's wrong with my face?"

"Look in a mirror, Stormy Weather Adrian."

We didn't have any mirrors in the store. He stared at me sullenly.

I asked, "Do you want the usual boring coffee, or are you feeling adventurous? I could get you a latte with two pumps of peppermint syrup and one pump of cinnamon. Rhonda calls it Christmas in July."

Adrian's expression, which had already been bitter, became worse. "Ew."

"Just the usual then," I said.

He reached into his pocket for some money.

"It's on me, boss," I said with a hand wave.

"I'm not your boss. I'm the operations manager."

"Whatever you say, *boss*." I opened the door and stepped back out into the refreshing sunshine.

It was always nice to duck out from underneath Adrian's storm clouds.

I had a skip in my step as I walked down the sidewalk.

The future home of Bookworm Books wasn't right next door to Donut Joe's anymore, but I liked that it was farther away because it gave me more of a break from Adrian when he was in one of his moods.

It had been less than a week since our Big Talk. On Monday of the previous week, he had spontaneously come clean about having kissed not just Brittany Brown but Sunshine Banks as well. The guy had great timing. I'd been prepared to dump him for his cheating ways when he'd told me about it, out of the blue. From the way Sunshine and Brittany had been carrying on, I'd assumed the physical contact had been a lot more than kissing. Adrian swore it wasn't, and I believed him.

He'd also told me about his new rat, Munchies, the three-legged fugitive from my neighbor Mr. Galloway's kitchen. He had been asked to "take care of" the rat, and rather than murder the poor thing, he'd paid for veterinary care and was now a pet rat owner. His father was disgusted with him, but I thought it was sweet.

With those secrets out of the way, everything should have been great between us. However, tensions had been growing, and the usual girlfriend techniques for releasing relationship tensions weren't doing much. Either I was losing my touch or something else was going on. Well, it had to be something else, because I had never been more on my game. I had a closet full of fancy underwear and wasn't afraid to use it.

Why was he still such a grump?

Was it the stress of moving the bookstore? That had to be it.

He couldn't still be upset about that silly—and completely false—story that I was dating Dalton Deangelo again. Adrian knew it wasn't true, plus he kept telling me it didn't bother him in the least.

I got to Donut Joe's, where I ordered a Christmas in July latte for myself and a boring plain one for Adrian. I also grabbed some of the lunch boxes with the boiled eggs that Adrian liked, a secret snack for later, and a small donut to eat on the way back to the bookstore. Okay, it was a regular-sized donut. It was not my fault the store only made them one size.

Rhonda wasn't working that day, so I didn't linger.

When I got back to the papered-over front of the bookstore, I had to battle my way through the line of people waiting to have brunch at Delilah's. They were like zombies. A hungry guy with red eyes and a gummy mouth tried to buy the boiled-egg lunch boxes from me while his friends laughed at him. I felt sorry for the guy, so I gave him the cranberry muffin I had stashed in my purse for later. His friends thought this was hilarious. The guy devoured the muffin and promised to be a regular and faithful customer at the bookstore when it opened later that month.

By the time I got inside the store and locked the door behind me, I was a solid half hour late for my shift.

Adrian said, "It's about time." He didn't say it in a snarky way, though. He said it in a light-hearted, joking way, like a boss in a sitcom.

"You'll have to dock my pay," I said.

"I will," he said. "I'll dock your pay by thirty-seven minutes."

"Speaking of pay, what's Mr. Olivier paying you, anyway?"

"I don't have an hourly rate."

"That's not what I asked."

He gave me a wary look. "It's not something we should be discussing. The operations manager has a lot of responsibilities. I get here early and stay late. If you added up my hours, I probably make less than you on an hourly basis."

"How much less? I want to know."

He smirked. "I know you do. That's why I'm not going to tell you."

"I'll get it out of you, one way or another."

He raised an eyebrow. "You think so, huh?"

I came around the refurbished counter we'd had delivered from the liquidation center the day of our hike and the bear attack. I pressed up against him as I set our takeout containers down. I gazed up at his icy-blue eyes and batted my eyelashes.

"Did you miss me?" I asked.

"When you were gone for twenty-one minutes? Yes. I missed you, Peaches Monroe. I was bereft. I sobbed my way through two silk handkerchiefs. I only just pulled myself together before you walked in."

"I knew it. Sometimes you get spoiled rotten from having me around too much, and I have to go away so you can miss me."

"Is that what happened?" He raised his eyebrows. "All I know is you go for a walk, and when you come back, you've got donut breath and your mood is much better."

"My mood? You're the grumpy one."

"I have a long face," he said plainly. "People think I'm sad or grumpy when I'm not. If you think there's a problem, it's you, Peaches. You project your moods onto me."

I laughed over how ridiculous that was. "What do you mean I have donut breath? That can't be. I haven't had a donut in ages." I breathed on my palm and sniffed it. To be honest, it did smell of cake and vanilla.

Adrian said, "I thought we were going to be honest with each other from now on."

"But what's the fun in sneaking a donut if I'm not really sneaking it?"

"You tell me." He wrapped his arms around me. "It's still fun being with you now, even though we're not sneaking around and hiding it from our parents like we did in high school."

"That was fun." I kissed him. "But this is fun, too."

He kissed me back then started tugging on my clothes.

"Adrian!"

"There's newspaper on the windows," he said.

"Beds exist for a reason," I said.

"Beds are for sleeping," he said. "What's the problem? Nobody can see us. Not unless they look really hard, between the seams."

"But people are *right* outside. They saw me come in here."

"So?"

He picked me up and set me on the counter so we were face to face and he didn't have to keep bending down to kiss me. He went back to putting the moves on me.

"Adrian," I said, struggling to maintain focus. "What if I didn't lock the door? Those people out there in line for brunch are hungry, and they saw me bring food in here. You know how people are in this neighborhood. They'll just open the door anyway and ask to use the washroom, or try to chat us up about what day the store will be open."

He kept kissing me on the neck. He was hungrier for my neck than the zombie guy outside had been for my cranberry muffin.

"We need to check the door," I said.

Adrian murmured, "I heard you lock it."

I pulled back. "Did you? Really?"

"I'm ninety-nine percent sure," he said.

"Good enough for me." I helped him get my shirt off.

Chapter 3

Saturday, August 6th (A month later)

In spite of Bookworm Books' very bossy operations manager, who was always getting distracted by a certain buxom employee, we managed to roll out a successful transition to the smaller location in July.

We weren't quite a full week into August, and the month was already shaping up to be the best August the store had enjoyed in over a decade.

The owner of the property and the business, Gordon Olivier, was delighted at how well the shop was doing. Almost as delighted as he was about the new specialty wine boutique that he—with help from Adrian Stromquist—would be opening in our former location.

"Baker Street is paved with gold," Gordon kept saying. "If you know how to dig."

One day when he said that, I brought up the idea of getting a raise. He stopped talking about how Baker Street was paved with gold. He did, however, give me a small raise.

Things were running smoothly at the new location.

That was, until the first Monday in August, when the store's computer spontaneously caught on fire.

I was working when it happened. I put out the fire with our fire extinguisher.

We were back up and running on Wednesday.

Sorry if that sounded like it was going to be more of a big anecdote than it was. I had been pretty surprised when the old computer had started smoking, but I can't say I was shocked. It was a pretty old system, and we'd been tempting fate for years.

Adrian bought one of those ozone machines and ran it while we were closed to take the smoke smell out of the space. The unit did the job it was advertised to do. What more can I say about the fire? It could have taken out the whole block, but it didn't. Sometimes bad luck is good luck.

The next exciting thing to happen in August happened on a Saturday.

My drama sensors alerted me the instant my dark-haired teenage employee, Garnet Langtree, walked in. He'd come with his own personal storm cloud over his head.

I asked, "What's wrong, kiddo?"

"Nothing," he said unconvincingly.

"Something's lurking over your head, Garnet. I haven't seen a gloomy localized weather pattern like that since I was in high school with our operations manager. We'd better call up that cute weatherman, Lance Philby, and report a local stormfront approaching."

"Not funny," Garnet said, glowering.

"It's not funny at all. First the fire, now this? What's next? A plague of locusts?"

Garnet continued glowering.

"Something's up," I said. "I haven't seen you this miserable since your mom cancelled a trip home to spend time with you-know-who." Garnet's mother, Jade, had visited a certain TV vampire at his Malibu treatment facility back in June. We didn't mention Dalton Deangelo by name in the store. It was a rule. We had a full page about it in the staff operations manual.

Garnet dropped his backpack on the floor with a thunk and stared at me. "I forgot about that."

"I'm sorry I reminded you," I said. "What did your mom do now?"

He looked over at the customers who were browsing the new arrivals and the magazines. That look told me his mother *had* done something, and that he didn't want to discuss it with customers in the store. She was a celebrity, so he had to be extra careful.

I waved for him to follow me out the back door. If the staff from Delilah's weren't having a cigarette break in the alley, we would have some privacy.

I opened the door. The coast was clear.

The bookstore was shaped like a bowling lane, so we'd be able to see everything going on from outside the back door. In some ways, the new store was superior to the original location, despite being half the size.

Garnet kicked his backpack under the counter and followed me out.

"So?" I asked him once we were both in the alley. "What did Jade do now?"

"It's not what she did *now*. She's actually been fine lately. It's about something she did seventeen years ago." He snorted. "Or some*one* she did seventeen years ago."

I felt a flare of excitement, but I kept it under control, out of respect for Garnet.

With restraint, I asked, "Is there news about your genetic father? Did she finally tell you who it was, or did you get a match from the DNA people?"

"I got a match," he said, his face twitching. "It's a sibling. Well, a half-sibling. I don't even know if it's a guy or a girl, because they haven't told me."

"Are you sure it's not your sister, Perry? A lot of people are sending their samples in out of curiosity."

He frowned. "Why would Perry send in her DNA? She knows who her dad is."

"Sometimes people do it to find out what parts of the world their ancestors are from. I don't know, Garnet. I'm just trying to help you out. I know you haven't told anyone but me about this, so I'm trying to do a good job and be, like, a responsible adult that you can count on." I wrinkled my nose. "Sort of."

He looked away and swept one hand through his dark hair. "It's not Perry," he said. "This other person and I had some emails back and forth, and it doesn't feel like Perry."

"So, what's next?"

"I don't know. Last night, I sent this person my picture, my first name, and my phone number."

"You did?" I couldn't control my curiosity. It came out as a double fist shake.

Garnet said, "Someone had to go first."

"And?"

Garnet angrily kicked an empty tomato sauce can that had escaped Delilah's recycling bin. The can rattled and clanged as it bounced down the alley.

"And *nothing*," Garnet said sullenly. "I haven't heard back."

That explained the local storm cloud.

"What a jerk," I said. "How dare they leave you hanging?"

"I know." Garnet looked around for something else to kick. There was only a pebble, and he kicked it. The pebble barely moved. He kicked it again. Still nothing.

I leaned down, picked up the pebble, and threw it hard down the alley.

That made Garnet's sour expression crack a little.

"You're going to be okay," I said, keeping my tone even while playing the role of the responsible adult friend. "Whoever your half sibling is, he or she is probably working up the courage to contact you. This sort of thing can be incredibly disruptive to a family. In our family, we have a rule that kids will be told everything they need to know once they're twelve, but what if this other person didn't have a family like that?"

"I shouldn't have sent a photo," Garnet said. He looked down at the alley's rough pavement. "They took one look at my dumb face and didn't want anything to do with me."

"Oh, Garnet." I tried to grab him for a motherly hug, but he quickly stepped back, evading capture.

"Don't try to cheer me up," he said. "I'm ugly, and I know it."

"You are not ugly," I said. "It's the rejection. Rejection makes you feel ugly, even when you aren't. It's like depression. Rejection lies."

He crossed his arms. "You're just saying that to make me feel better."

"Maybe. But you're also a handsome little devil, and you know it."

His cheeks reddened. He was a good-looking kid, and he did know it.

I glanced back into the store. One of the browsing customers was headed toward the checkout counter.

"We will discuss this later," I said to Garnet. "Though I really wish you'd talked to your dad about this whole thing before you sent in your sample."

"He's not my dad," Garnet said, pouting.

"You wouldn't say that if he was here. I've met your dad. Dale Langtree is a good man, and he is your father no matter what."

Garnet had let his guard down, so I was able to grab him for one quick hug.

Then I ran back into the store to ring up the customer's sale on our new, less flammable computer.

Chapter 4

By four o'clock that Saturday, Garnet still hadn't heard back from his mysterious relative. He was still in a funk, but it didn't seem as deep. He agreed with me that it could take months for the other person to get brave enough to make contact, and that checking his email every two minutes was not going to speed up the process.

The store had gotten quiet, and it was the end of my shift, so I prepared to leave. Garnet would run things the last few hours and close up.

I grabbed my purse and said, "Don't let anything catch on fire while I'm gone."

He replied, "Things only catch on fire when you're here, Peaches."

"That's because I know how to use a fire extinguisher."

"I don't think that's how fire works."

I headed for the back door, then changed my mind and went out the front.

The brunch line for Delilah's, the busy restaurant next door, had evaporated. I slowed down and waved at the staff inside. One of the waitresses was Garnet's sister, Peridot Langtree. She was at the front, cleaning kids' handprints off the glass. She pretended to spray me through the glass, and I pretended she'd gotten me right in the eye.

Baker Street wasn't literally paved with gold, as Gordon Olivier had described it, but the street was populated with a lot of great people. Baker Street was like a cozy small town within a big city. People who lived or worked in the neighborhood got to enjoy the best of both worlds.

I reached the location of my boss's new specialty wine store, which was to be called Bumblebee

Booze. The name had started out as a joke, as a twist on the previous business, Bookworm Books, but then nobody on the team had been able to come up with anything better.

The more traditional-minded folks in the neighborhood were horrified about having the word *booze* in the store name. Why not *spirits*? Or *liquor*? Or something more upscale, like *fine wines and ale*? When confronted by people with that opinion, Mr. Olivier would calmly mention that his second choice had been Humdinger Hooch. That usually got people on board with the name Bumblebee Booze. Plus the logo, a giant, friendly-looking bee, was adorable.

The front door was locked, so I knocked and yelled through the papered-over glass that it was me.

Adrian opened the door and greeted me with a hug. He looked sweaty, and he smelled worse. I couldn't help but recoil and wrinkle my nose dramatically.

"What's the matter?" He sniffed his armpit. "Uh, never mind. I'm not exactly fresh as a daisy."

"You've been working hard." I looked around at all the new display shelves. "It's really coming together." I went over to the checkout counter to admire the new computer. "Everything's brand-spanking new. This booze shop is clearly Gordon's favorite child. When it comes to the bookstore, if I want any computer equipment that's less than a decade old, I have to set the old stuff on fire."

Adrian gave me a wary look. "I thought that computer fire was accidental?"

"It *was* an accident."

"Are you sure about that? Or is it like when your cousin Megan happened to be near Howard Hamilton's car when it caught on fire?"

"Megan did not set Howard Hamilton's car on fire. That would be crazy."

Adrian pressed his lips flat. "It sure would be. Speaking of Howard, he's coming by any minute now to go over some spreadsheets for the cash flow." Howard Hamilton was my cousin Megan's ex-boyfriend. He had been handling the accounting for all of Gordon Olivier's businesses for years.

"He's coming now? For how long?"

Adrian shrugged. "For a few hours. For as long as it takes."

"What about dinner? You said you'd take me to Niro's."

"I said I *might* be able to swing it."

I made a noise to let him know I was disappointed. My body felt heavy, and the bottoms of my feet were sore.

"Don't have one of your tantrums," he said.

"My *what*?"

"You're making that disappointed face," he said smugly. "I can always tell you're on the verge of freaking out."

"This is just how my face looks. If you think I'm on the verge of freaking out, then you must be projecting your own issues at me."

His nostrils flared. He leaned back on a sawdust-covered workbench. "Is this how it's always going to be between us?"

"Only when I think we have a date for Saturday night and then it turns out we don't."

"Even if I do finish early with Howard, I can't go anywhere looking and smelling like this. How about I pick up some takeout from Niro's and bring it over to your house later?"

"Sure," I said flatly. "Nisha's have Noah over tonight. You and Noah can drink light beer all night, and you can ignore me like you did last Saturday."

The corner of his mouth hitched up in a know-it-all grin. "You're kind of hard to ignore," he said.

"And yet you manage to do it whenever Noah is around. You two are way too into each other. It's weird."

"You should be happy I get along with your best friend's boyfriend. That would be the normal thing to do."

"Adrian, sometimes it feels like—"

I was interrupted by a knock at the door.

"That'll be Howard," Adrian said, jumping up to open the door for the accountant.

Howard came in, dressed in a summer-weight suit. He was carrying both a briefcase and a laptop bag.

"Hello, Ms. Monroe," Howard said in his nerdy voice. "I heard there was a fire at the bookstore."

"It wasn't too bad," I said. "Almost no damage, except to the computer. It was a very precise fire."

"Funny how that happens sometimes," Howard said. "It's interesting how spontaneous combustions tend to occur around certain members of your family."

I gave him a stony face. "I don't know what you're talking about," I lied. Everyone knew about Megan and the incident with Howard's car.

Howard said, "In any case, congratulations on your great numbers at the new location for Bookworm Books." Howard shot a grin at Adrian. "I'm sure it will be nice to not hemorrhage money for a while." He glanced up at the gleaming new lights that would illuminate Bumblebee's selection of fine wines, ales, and more. "This new place should do quite nicely for Mr. Olivier."

Adrian said, "That's the plan, Howard. Thanks for coming by. I'd shake your hand, but I've been sawing a lot of wood today, and I'm liable to transfer one of my many slivers to you."

"That's all right," Howard said. "I don't like shaking hands anyway." He gave me a wary look. "Are you joining us, Ms. Monroe?"

"Don't get too excited," I said. "I only popped in to say hi to my boyfriend."

Howard gave me a blank look. "And who's that?"

I gave Adrian a dirty look. "He doesn't know?"

Adrian gave me a look as blank as Howard's.

I felt a familiar tension in my shoulders and heat flash through me. I'd felt that way so many times in high school, thanks to Adrian. He'd been so cool to me in public, but a completely different person in private.

I shouldn't have said anything in front of the accountant, but I was already agitated about dinner.

"Old habits die hard, huh?" I spat out the words. "Are you still embarrassed about being with me, Adrian? We're not in high school anymore."

Howard watched me out of the corners of his eyes.

Adrian gave me a tired look. "Peaches, I've been talking to Howard about the line of credit and other financial matters. We don't exactly chat about our love lives."

Howard's head bobbed to the side in surprise. "We don't? But I told you about the wedding, and about Charlotte's family, and..." Howard trailed off and wisely began looking for a clean space to open his briefcase and laptop bag.

Adrian said to me, "I'm not keeping anything a secret. If anyone asks me directly, I tell them the truth."

"Which is what?"

"That I have a girlfriend." He started walking toward me slowly. "And that her name is Peaches." He closed the distance between us and wrapped his arms around me. "And that we're crazy about each other. So crazy that she doesn't even mind it when I smell bad."

I pretended to try to get away from him, but not very hard. Even when he was sweaty, Adrian still smelled good to me. We'd always had chemistry on our side. It was the chemistry between us that had gotten me in trouble.

Another old high school feeling returned. My knees were weak. I didn't feel heavy or tired anymore. In Adrian's arms, I felt like he was the only thing keeping me from floating away.

Howard muttered to himself as he located a working outlet for his laptop power cord.

Adrian kissed me chastely on the forehead. "See you later," he said huskily.

"You'd better shower before you come to my place tonight."

"Why?" He pulled his head back and gave me an innocent look. "You're just going to make me sweaty all over again."

"Fine. Don't shower. But I'm going to sniff you at the front door, and possibly spray you down in the front yard with the garden hose."

He grinned. "That sounds fun."

"Once the water that's been standing in the hose drains out, it gets cold fast. Really cold."

"I can withstand a little abuse," he said. "I might even enjoy the abuse. I guess that's why I like being with you."

I rolled my eyes, gave him a peck on the cheek, and left him to his meeting with Howard Hamilton.

Chapter 5

Seconds after saying goodbye to one tall, attractive man, I stepped out of the future wine store and nearly got run over by a different one.

It was Luca Lowell, my cousin Tina's husband and the owner of Ralph's Garage. Luca was as tall as Adrian but much beefier. He had friendly eyes and sandy-brown hair with a natural curl. He worked on motorbikes, and he looked like he lifted them over his head for lunchtime exercise.

Luca apologized for nearly turning me into a pancake. "I've been running around like a headless chicken, trying to get everything ready before we head out of town," he said.

Tina and Luca hadn't gone for a honeymoon directly after their wedding due to summer being the busy season at the garage, with everyone getting their motorbikes on the road for the season. The two newlyweds would be leaving for a big world tour in September.

I asked, "How are things going at the garage?" He'd been running Ralph's for about a year.

"Busier than ever," he replied. "But in a good way. I can't complain. How's the new bookstore?"

"Also busier than ever," I said. "You know what's funny? The number of people who come in and say it's about time there was a bookstore on Baker Street. People who've lived in the neighborhood for years. I tell them we've been on this street forever, and they stare at me like I'm making it up for my own amusement. I've gotten into arguments with people about it. Can you believe it?"

"I believe it," Luca said, grinning and rubbing his sandy-brown beard. "People still come into the garage and ask if I'm Ralph. And these are people who have been around the neighborhood long enough to have known Ralph." He shook his head. "The guys at the shop got me a set of overalls with Ralph embroidered on the chest. It was just a gag gift, but I keep wearing them because they're my best overalls."

We both laughed, then I said, "Soon you'll get a break from the role of Ralph. I'm sure you two will have an amazing honeymoon."

"Being anywhere with Tina is amazing," he said. Luca was the sort of guy who said romantic things like that. He'd wooed Tina by getting her a bracelet with meaningful symbols on the charms. Tina was a lucky girl.

He pointed at me. "Hey, when's that ad campaign coming out? Both Tina and Megan have been bragging to anyone who'll listen about their supermodel cousin."

"The campaign comes out in print next month," I said. "The magazines are first, then an online campaign."

"I can't wait," he said. "The guys at the shop want you to come by for autographs."

"Yeah, right!" I laughed.

"I'm serious," he said. "People think it's a big deal to be in a national ad campaign."

"It's international," I said.

Luca grinned. "See? Don't tell me you aren't looking forward to all the attention."

"I don't know. It's hard to wrap my head around the whole thing."

"You'll make an excellent celebrity, Peaches Monroe. I know it."

"Thanks."

Luca looked over my shoulder, at the paper-covered door of the wine shop. "Is Adrian in there?"

"He sure is. He's meeting with the accountant."

"Howard is here, too? That's handy. Gotta love Baker Street." Luca reached for the door but didn't open it yet. "I was talking to Adrian at the family barbecue last month about doing some work for me once the wine shop is up and running. I'm planning an expansion, since we can't keep up with demand in the current space. How is he as an operations manager? Honestly?"

"He gets distracted easily," I said.

Luca's friendly eyes widened with surprise. "Really?"

"He only gets distracted by little ol' me." I punched Luca on the shoulder. "That shouldn't be a problem for you, big guy."

"But he's good at what he does, right?"

I squared up my shoulders and stood tall. "Adrian Stromquist has a near-genius IQ. He's much stronger than he looks. He can do anything he sets his mind to and would be a fine addition to any team."

"He sounds like a real catch. Do you love him?"

"Luca! That's girl talk. Don't be weird."

He gave me a smile as big as his muscular shoulders. "Big, strong guys have feelings, too. If you ever want to talk, I'm around. We're family now."

I thanked him and told him to have a good meeting with Adrian and Howard. I hadn't realized Luca knew Howard, but it made sense that those two did business together, since Howard did the accounting for Tina and Megan's florist business. Baker Street was a small world.

As I walked back to the house, I thought about Luca's question.

Did I love Adrian Stromquist?

I did enjoy spending time with him... when we weren't bickering. There was less bickering when the clothes came off. When it came to the physical stuff, Adrian truly was excellent at anything he set his mind on. He had learned a lot since high school—not that he hadn't already showed great promise back then.

As for love, I didn't know. Nobody had asked me that question so directly. I hadn't even asked myself.

Perhaps it was too soon to say. We'd known each other as kids, then I hadn't seen him for years. We'd only seen each other again that summer, in early May. The official start of our current relationship was June twentieth. That was the first time we'd actually kissed, among other things. It was only August sixth now, so we hadn't even been together a full two months.

Who knew they were in love after only two months?

As I asked myself that question, I had the answer.

Luca Lowell had known.

According to him, he'd fallen in love with my cousin Tina the instant he'd seen her in Gardenia Flowers. It had been love at first sight—for Luca, anyway. The women in my family had eaten up that particular story. As far as they were concerned, big, strong Luca was perfect. He had hung the moon and the stars in the sky.

It must have been easy for Tina to fall in love with him. Luca was quite the catch. He did tease people— Tina about the very small cottage she insisted they live in, and Megan about her relationship with Muffins, the cat—but Luca was always smiling and relaxed, and his jokes never seemed mean.

Adrian, on the other hand, was not like Luca. He had a defensive streak.

Just that afternoon, when I'd dropped in to see him at the wine store, what should have been a pleasant visit had come dangerously close to another argument. He was so unwilling to bend or admit to anything on his part. He had made plans with me for dinner at Niro's. Firm plans. Then, rather than apologize to me for bailing on the plans we'd made, he'd turned it around and insinuated that I was the difficult one.

Was I difficult? Probably. But didn't my other positive traits add up to much more than my flaws?

I wanted him to appreciate me for who I was, how I was. It would be nice if I could fall in love with him, but I needed to know he felt the same way about me. It was probably something he was doing that was preventing me from knowing I was in love with him.

Never mind how I felt about him.

When would Adrian Stromquist fall in love with *me*?

Chapter 6

Nisha elbowed her way through the crowd of people inside the bookstore and set a pair of takeout cups on the counter.

I clapped my hands with excitement. I'd known she was coming because she'd sent me a text message, but her appearance still felt like a surprise. I felt slightly dizzy, and my fingers were tingling. Everything felt right in the world whenever my best friend showed up at my workplace with a treat. Life's pleasures could be so simple.

Nisha eyed the assortment of shoppers and browsers. "Are you sure you have time for a coffee break? It's pretty busy in here."

"These are all regulars," I said. "They won't have any questions or need anything from me until they're ready to buy a book or two."

"Is it the size of the store making it look like more people than it is? I swear you never used to have this many regulars on a Saturday before."

"It's more," I said.

"Why would a smaller store attract more people?"

"Good question, easy answer. We used to be next door to Donut Joe's, which never had a line for brunch, on account of how they don't serve brunch. Now we're next door to Delilah's, which is a magnet for people who have nothing better to do on a Saturday morning. Even before Delilah's opens, those dummies are standing around on the sidewalk, waiting for a table so they can get adequate diner food with top-level abuse by the waitresses in there."

Nisha nodded and looked over the crowd. "If they're out there for hours, it makes sense they might get curious about books. But won't they lose their place in line if they come in here?"

"They all take turns and save each other's spots. It's quite the system. Before we opened up here, Adrian and I figured we might have to put a selection of books on the sidewalk to draw people in. It turns out that wasn't necessary. I could put a sign on the door saying we only sell fish bait on the weekend, and people would still come in."

"I'm glad it's working out," Nisha said.

We both raised our takeout cups. "To things working out," I said.

She smiled and took a sip.

"When do you need to be back at the booze shop?" I asked.

"Not for another fifteen minutes," she said.

Nisha was no longer unemployed. She had been hired by Gordon Olivier, on Adrian's recommendation, to manage Baker Street's most notorious—and *only*—fine wines and ale shop. Adrian had been interviewing candidates for days when he realized there was a highly competent—and available—manager right under his nose. Before Nisha had quit her last job, she had practically run Noah's yoga studio, plus she did have a business management degree from college.

Nisha's life had really changed over the summer. She'd started out with zero love life and a stalled career. She'd been pining over her boss while running his business for a third of what she should have been getting paid.

All it had taken to change everything was for her to quit the job. Then Noah finally realized what he'd had. She didn't go back to working for him at the studio, but she did finally get what she'd really wanted all along—Noah. I wasn't the biggest fan of the guy, but he was growing on me.

"How are things with Noah?" I asked. "I heard a lot of giggling in your bedroom last night."

"It's going so well," she said breathlessly. "Ever since I made him prawns vindaloo, everything has changed. He started eating all sorts of seafood, and eggs, and even beef. He's seeing my herbalist now, and she says the whole problem was that his cholesterol was too low because he didn't eat anything but greens and rice. He was so proud of his low numbers, even though he felt like death on melba toast. Did you know the body makes hormones out of cholesterol, and every cell wall in your body is made from cholesterol?"

"Enough of your weird woo-woo energy and witchcraft talk," I said with a hand wave. "Next thing I know, you'll be telling me that eating donuts while cursing at people on social media is bad for me."

She rolled her eyes.

A male customer in a T-shirt and a lightweight scarf came over with a couple of cookbooks. His name was Ryan, and he always wore a scarf, no matter what the weather was like. He also had a phobia about escalators and other mechanically moving surfaces. The solution to Ryan's problem was obvious to everyone but Ryan. We'd had a few discussions about his issues. After I read a popular book by a psychologist—which basically made me an expert—I'd determined that Ryan was a *help-seeking complainer* who liked getting attention for his misfortunes. But he was a nice enough guy, other than the scarf-escalator thing. So what if he had one weird thing he couldn't fix? It took all types to make the world go 'round.

I rang up the cookbooks.

Ryan said, "Why am I always so hungry whenever I'm in here? I swear I keep buying these cookbooks just because of the food on the cover."

"You *are* buying them for the pictures on the cover," I said. "And you're always hungry because you come in hungover every Saturday morning while you're waiting two hours to get brunch at Delilah's."

The guy grinned. "That's probably it."

"Plus, Ryan, you sold me your soul for the price of one cranberry muffin."

"Was that legally binding? I don't think we even shook hands."

"I own you," I said, shaking my finger at him. "You should be more careful about what you agree to from now on. And don't sign any NDAs without having your dad read them thoroughly."

"Will do," the young man said.

After Ryan left, Nisha said, "Do you always talk to the customers like that?"

"Just the Saturday morning regulars. They love the abuse. Plus Ryan is a special case."

She raised one dark eyebrow. "He's special, all right."

"And single," I said. "Can you believe it? People say the good ones are always taken, but it's not true."

She snorted. "I don't know. He's kinda cute. The scarf is weird."

"You shouldn't even be looking at other boys. Aren't you and Noah deeply in love?"

"No," she said casually.

"No? You're not in love?"

"Nope," she said. "I do care about him, but it's not capital-L Love."

"But you were infatuated with him for ages. You were in love with him from afar while he was chasing after skinny blondes. And now you two have been dating longer than Adrian and I have been. How are you not in love?"

"We just aren't." She tucked some of her silky black hair behind her ear. Nisha had recently cut her long, beautiful tresses into a shoulder-length bob. Her hair looked spectacular, and shinier than ever.

She stared at me and asked, "Are you and Adrian in love?"

"I don't know," I said. "It's too soon to say."

She smirked as she turned the tables on me. "Ah, but you guys have known each other since you were kids. How much longer is it going to take?"

"Funny you should ask. I have the answer right here." I pulled out a paperback I'd been reading behind the counter when the store was slow and I didn't have a friend to gossip with. It was a revised, expanded, and updated edition of *The Secret Rules of Love*. One of the co-authors, Dottie Simpkins, had autographed my copy herself.

"Ooh," Nisha said. "The new edition." Nisha had dragged me to one of Dottie's workshops earlier that summer.

"I got you a signed copy for Christmas, but you can have yours now if you don't want to wait until December."

"I'll wait," she said. "What does the book say?"

I opened it to my bookmark and showed her a diagram of the human brain. All the major parts were labeled.

"I don't get it," Nisha said.

"It's brain science," I said. "This is the start of the new, updated section where Dottie consulted a bunch of neuroscientists about love. Long story short, there are two kinds of romantic feelings. Dopamine feelings and serotonin feelings."

Nisha gave me a skeptical look. "And you're the one who shuts me down for woo-woo talk if I mention hormones and cell walls?"

"Only because I'm uncomfortable hearing about your boyfriend's issues raising the ol' flagpole," I said. "I have an extremely vivid imagination. Even if you use the most general terms, I picture everything." I stuck out my tongue. "Ew. Noah."

"Oh, Peaches."

"Anyway, Dottie and her brain guru said that if it's really love, you'll know after a year."

Nisha took the book from my hand and skimmed to the end. Not only was she a book-ruiner who read the last page first but she also burned through books at too high a speed to truly savor them.

"I see," Nisha said. "This one-year thing is only about determining if it's meant to last. You don't have to wait a year to *start* feeling love."

"You don't?" I hadn't gotten that far in the book, or I'd missed something.

"Of course not," she said. "Waiting a year to start feeling something sounds like what my parents would say if they were banging on about arranged marriages again."

"Oh." I put the book away. "Then never mind."

We stared at each other quietly for a moment.

Another customer came up with some literary novels by a respected author. Nisha stepped aside. I rang up the sale and congratulated the customer for having better taste than ninety percent of our customers.

After the customer left, Nisha said, "Why did you say that? You hate that author."

"I do. I hate him with a fiery passion. But only because I have terrible taste in books."

Nisha made her eating-sour-foods face.

I said, "Don't look at me like that. I can be objective about my own trash tendencies."

"Right," she said with an eyeroll. "You're the most objective person I know." She started backing away. "Time's up. Back to slinging booze under the big bumblebee sign. If you refer some people over to me, I'll give them free samples."

"I thought you guys only did that when the brand ambassadors were doing a promotion."

She held up both hands. "Are you suggesting I should have to drink alone? Just because I'm at work?"

A few of my book customers looked up at Nisha with interest.

"She's joking," I told the customers.

Nisha held her hand to her mouth and stage-whispered on her way out, "Totally *not* joking!"

Chapter 7

I had just finished the coffee Nisha had brought me when Garnet arrived for his shift.

He tucked his backpack under the counter, said hello at me, and went straight for a stack of graphic novels that had just arrived. Without looking up from the artwork, he asked, "How's it been today?"

"Steady," I said. "We sold a lot of daybooks and planners for all the kids going back to school."

He looked up. "Oh. I should get one before they're all gone."

"Are you excited about getting back to school? Grade eleven is an exciting year."

"I guess so," he said.

"Any news from your, um, online friend?" I was referring to the half-sibling he'd been matched with through a DNA analysis site but hadn't met yet.

"Weirdly, yes. It's a girl. She won't say who our father is, but she dropped some big hints that she definitely knows. She wants to tell me in person."

"And you're sure it's not Perry messing with you?"

"Yeah. I'm sure." He flicked his hand through his dark hair in a familiar gesture. Garnet reminded me of someone, but I couldn't put my finger on who. "The girl sent me a picture from when she was younger." He stuffed his hands in his pockets. "She's cute."

"That's..." I was at a loss for words. One did not want to find one's half-sibling "cute."

His cheeks reddened. "So, obviously, I can't see her. I mean, what if I like her in the wrong way? That can happen. There's a big warning on the website about it."

"Yikes," I said, which was the appropriate reaction for such a colossal *yikes* scenario. "Garnet, it might be time for you to finally talk to your dad about this."

"I did," he said.

"Good," I said with relief. I was glad to no longer be the only adult who knew about Garnet's predicament. "How did that go?"

Garnet looked down and kicked invisible dirt. "He was really disappointed, but he wasn't surprised. Back when he got me tested, he didn't take the option to find relatives, but he knew about it."

"What did he say? Did he freak out?"

"He called a family meeting with all of us, including my mom. That did *not* go well."

I crossed my arms. "If your silly mom would just tell you who the guy was, none of this confusing stuff would have to happen."

Garnet looked away, his cheeks growing even more red. "At the family meeting, she told us she's not sure. She said she could make a short list with a few names, but she'd only give them to me when she felt I was ready. She said I should wait until I'm eighteen."

I took in a big breath with that bombshell. "I know she's your mom, but *a short list*? As in multiple options? Talk about a flaming bag of poo. I'm so sorry, kiddo."

He shrugged. "She's bluffing. She knows exactly who it is. She's messing with me, trying to get me to back off."

"Let's hope so," I said. "Even if it is just a bluff to buy her more time, that's still a flaming bag of poo."

"It is." He picked up the graphic novel and went back to reading it.

A minute passed. Garnet's attention was entirely on the book. It was a popular series.

"Good talk," I said. "I'm glad we got that all sorted out."

"Yeah," he said distractedly.

"I'm doing fine," I said. "Thanks for asking about my personal life."

"Yeah," he said again. "Good."

I patted him on the shoulder. "Never change, Garnet."

He glanced up and gave me a confused look. "What?"

"When you're done reading that graphic novel, there are a few more customers to be called for their special orders. Everything's marked with Post-Its."

"Post-Its," he said. "Gotcha."

I gathered my things and went out the front door in search of my boyfriend.

He wasn't at the wine store, so I continued along the street to Ralph's Garage.

Chapter 8

I found Adrian at Ralph's Garage, having a beer in the back office with the owner, my cousin's husband, Luca Lowell. The office was not the typical garage office. It served as a sort of gentleman's lounge, where Luca entertained some of the shop's clientele. There was a desk and a computer and filing cabinets, but also leather chairs and sturdy tables made from motorbike parts and reclaimed wood.

Luca jumped up from his leather chair and offered me a beverage from the small refrigerator. Adrian remained seated, his long legs stretched out languidly in front of him. Both he and Cujo had a tendency to stretch out like that.

Did I want an adult beverage? I checked the time. It was just past two.

"I'm not sure it's beer o'clock just yet," I said.

Luca held an unopened bottle of microbrewery ale to his chest and grinned. "If you're too good for day drinking now that you're a famous underwear model..."

I grabbed the bottle from his hand. "Enough crazy talk. I'll never be too good for day drinking." I went over to the wall-mounted bottle opener—a miniature moose head—and cracked it open.

Adrian spoke to me for the first time since I'd walked in. He said, "That's a new beer we just got in at Bumblebee. Let me know what you think."

I took a drink. "It's cold and wet," I said. "Therefore, it fits my minimum requirements for day drinking."

Adrian raised an eyebrow. "Anything else?"

I took another swig then wiped my mouth with the back of my hand. "It's a bit too hoppy for my liking."

"People are into hoppy beer," he said, his brow furrowing the way it did when he was latching on for an argument.

"This is exactly why I don't give you my opinion about beer or wine," I said. "You always try to argue with my taste buds."

Adrian snorted. "What taste buds? I've seen you eat a Cheetos sandwich."

Luca chuckled. "Really?"

I put my free hand on my hip. "We were out of orange cheese, and I needed to pack a lunch."

"It's called cheddar," Adrian said, lifting his nose in the air. "Orange cheese is called *cheddar*."

I took a long drink of my beer then said snippily, "Thank you for correcting me, Mr. Stromquist."

"Don't be like that," Adrian said, his icy-blue eyes growing chilly.

"You could always try not constantly nitpicking everything I say."

Adrian's right eye twitched. "You could try not being wrong about everything."

Luca, who was still standing, held up two large hands. "That's enough, you two." He waved to an empty leather chair. "Peaches, are you going to relax and join us? You're welcome to hang out. We were just going over the plans for the expansion."

I walked over to the chair and looked at Adrian. His eye was still twitching. He didn't want me to stay. He seemed to enjoy hanging out with me one-on-one, but whenever we were in a group together, or even around one other person, he seemed to resent me being there. The first of my magazine ads were coming out that month, and I'd been getting more attention than usual, and that hadn't sat well with him. He didn't want to talk about it, either.

Luca was still waiting, looking uncomfortable. Luca didn't like conflict. He was a big, easygoing peace maker.

Rather than sit down, I chugged the rest of the beer and then put the empty with the collection on the windowsill.

"Thanks for the refreshment," I said to Luca, ignoring Adrian. "I'll be on my way so I don't slow down your meeting. I know you have a lot to figure out before you take Tina on that amazing honeymoon. She's a special lady, and I know you want to treat her right." I shot a look at Adrian. I knew he wouldn't react, and he didn't.

Luca said, "Nice of you to stop by, Peaches. And I appreciate the ringing endorsement you gave me for this guy." He nodded at Adrian then came over and gave me a big bear hug—with Luca, all hugs were bear hugs. "Thanks for letting me borrow him for a while."

"Keep him as long as you want," I said.

Out of the corner of my eye, I saw Adrian narrowing his eyes at me.

"This little project of mine should only take him a month," Luca said. "Then he can move on to the next thing."

"I'm sure he'll like that," I said. "Adrian enjoys jumping from one challenge to the next."

Luca asked, "Isn't that a good thing for a person?"

I could feel Adrian's gaze on me.

"Challenging yourself *is* important," I said. "Lots of people get excited about starting something, but not everyone is cut out for sticking around and dealing with the mess after the novelty is over."

Luca nodded. "Like running a business day to day." He took a deep breath into his big chest and said, "That's an entirely different skill set." Then he grinned. "Luckily for me, I don't need Adrian to run things here, so it's not going to be a problem for me when he's ready to move on to the next challenge."

"Then you two are perfect for each other," I said. "You two and your hoppy beer should be very happy together."

Luca clapped me on the shoulder with one big hand. "You're funny," he said. "If you ever get tired of the bookstore, I'd be happy to put you to work here."

"I don't know the first thing about cars, or bikes, or changing the oil in anything. I'm not entirely sure what motor oil is."

Luca winked at me. "I'd find something in your lane."

"You're the best," I said. "Tina's a lucky lady."

He grinned and wished me a good day as I went on my way.

Chapter 9

After I left the garage, I went by Donut Joe's to say hi to Rhonda. I was dying to complain to someone about Adrian. Everyone in my family thought he was the perfect boyfriend, but Rhonda was just cynical enough about men in general to believe me when I aired my grievances.

Rhonda was finishing her shift when I walked in.

"Where are you heading?" I asked.

"Home to my cat," she said, folding up her apron.

"Would your cat be offended if I took you to O'Flannigan's for a drink?"

"Yes, but she is forgiving, thanks to her short attention span."

"Plus it is Saturday night," I said.

Rhonda tilted her head to the side. "It's Saturday afternoon, Peaches." She leaned forward and sniffed. "Do I detect a beer aroma on your breath? You smell hoppy."

"I had one beer," I said. "It's Saturday night *somewhere*."

"You're not wrong." Rhonda grabbed her purse and gave me an excited grin. "Are we really doing this? Are we both ready to take our relationship to the next level?"

Rhonda and I had chatted for hours over the last year, mostly at the donut counter, or in the alley while she smoked, and occasionally at the bookstore.

"Let's do this," I said with a laugh. "Let's hang out together, just the two of us, without a counter between us or a dumpster next to us."

She laughed her gravelly laugh as we headed out of Donut Joe's together.

When we got to O'Flannigan's, we chose two chairs at the bar, on the corner.

Rhonda patted the bar counter and said in her gravelly voice, "I suppose it's for the best that we have a little bit of counter between us."

"You're right," I agreed. "We wouldn't want to take things too fast and then have regrets."

"Speaking of regrets..." Rhonda dug around in her large purse.

My heart began to pound. My mouth went dry.

Rhonda pulled out a magazine.

The pub noise faded to the background. My vision was blurry at the edges. All I could see or hear was my friend.

Rhonda said, "I'll regret it if I don't get your autograph." She opened the magazine to an image of me posing in a diamond necklace, peach-colored underwear, and nothing else.

The image was a shock to my eyes, even though I'd suspected it was coming the moment she'd started digging around in her purse.

I made a croaking sound.

"Aren't you cute," Rhonda said, looking at me and smiling. "Did you think people weren't going to see it? Honey, they didn't pay you all that money for nothing."

"This is my first time," I said, waving my fingers at my face. "I mean, I've seen the picture already, of course. I got a box of the magazines sent to my house, and we carry this one at Bookworm Books, but this is my first time encountering it out in the wild. Plus nobody's actually asked for my autograph until now." I kept waving my hands. There was a pleasant tingling sensation that started at the back of my head and radiated through me.

Rhonda dug around in her purse for something else.

My mouth was still dry, and I was suddenly very warm.

The beer I'd rapidly consumed back at Luca's garage had been relaxing me already, but this new feeling I was experiencing was the opposite. Everything was clashing inside me, and my thoughts turned to chaos.

Then it lifted, and I was on top of the world.

Any lingering annoyance I'd been feeling over Adrian and the prospect of another boyfriendless Saturday night was completely gone. Why would I care that my boyfriend would rather hang out with his friends than take me out? It didn't matter. I was above regular mortal worries now. I was a goddess in lace, immortalized in a popular magazine.

"I'm glad your first time was with me," Rhonda said as she handed me a felt-tipped pen. "Just sign your name anywhere."

As I took the pen I remembered my conversation with Mitchell, the brand manager I'd made friends with in Los Angeles. He'd warned me I would be asked for autographs, and that when it happened, I couldn't just sign my name the way I would on a boring legal document. My signature was my brand, and it had to have a look. It needed, as Mitchell put it, *panache*.

I tentatively drew a large, comically oversized P, then the rest of my name in bubbly, round letters. It was my regular handwriting, but better. Like how the image was me, but better, thanks to great lighting and expert retouching.

Rhonda took the magazine back and blew on the fresh ink.

The bartender who'd been standing nearby, chopping limes, stopped what he was doing and leaned over. He was new to the pub, and we didn't know each other. His eyes went wide as he looked from the magazine ad to me and back again. "Is that you?"

Rhonda answered for me. "It sure is." She held up the magazine for him to see.

"Wow." The bartender gave me an appreciative look. "You drink for free tonight."

Rhonda cleared her throat.

"You *and* your mom," the bartender said, smiling at Rhonda.

"She's my friend," I said to the man, correcting him.

Rhonda waved one hand. "I don't mind. At least he didn't say I was your grandma."

The bartender asked, "What'll it be? Please don't make me get out the blender and regret my offer."

Rhonda and I looked at each other and shrugged.

"I already had a beer," I said to the bartender. "What would you recommend for a Saturday afternoon?"

"Scotch," he said without hesitation. He was cute. There was something about a man providing a simple, succinct answer to a woman's question that was downright sexy. It was the opposite of how Adrian answered questions.

"Scotch it is," I replied. Rhonda answered similarly.

The bartender held out his hand for the magazine. "Do you mind if I show this to the kitchen? They'll kill me if they find out a celebrity was here and I didn't tell them."

"Oh, I'm not exactly a celeb—"

Rhonda thrust the magazine at him. "Be my guest."

The bartender tucked the magazine under his arm, poured us two generous glasses of amber booze, then disappeared.

O'Flannigan's was quiet enough that Rhonda and I were able to hear the kitchen staff whooping it up over my picture.

Rhonda said to me, "You're a celebrity now. Get used to it."

"Give me a minute," I said.

"How's the scotch?"

I took a sip. "Nice, I think." I set down the glass and leaned in. "Honestly, I can't taste anything right now. I can't even tell up from down. Am I leaning over right now? Like tilting to the side? Rhonda, please don't let me fall off my barstool."

"You *are* tilting to one side." She put her hands on my shoulders and corrected me. "There you go, Ms. Famous Underwear Model." She grabbed her cigarettes from her purse. "Now, if you'll excuse me, I have to go locate the designated area for me to you-know-what."

I started to get up from my chair, but she held up one hand to stop me.

"Relax," she said. "I'll be back in a jiffy. You can stay here with the drinks."

I stayed on the barstool while Rhonda left to smoke.

I wasn't alone for long. The kitchen staff started coming out, one at a time, to gawk at me. They were shy and kept ducking behind the bar's vertical beams.

"Don't be scared," I said, waving for them to stop hiding.

Soon, I was surrounded by men of all ages, dressed in kitchen whites, asking me what it was like to be a model.

"Keeping up my figure isn't easy," I said. "I have to eat a lot of chicken wings." I batted my eyelashes. "Speaking of which, is it too early to order dinner appetizers?"

I knew it was two hours too early to get the pub's famous chicken wings, but I had to try.

Three of the kitchen staff tripped over each other rushing to get back to the kitchen to make me some chicken wings.

"With the blue cheese dip," I called after them.

By the time Rhonda returned, we had an assortment of food showing up for us.

The kitchen staff were eventually cleared away when the pub owner, Gary Jackson, came by to see what the fuss was about. Mr. Jackson took one look at the magazine photo then spent a solid ten minutes staring at my chest in real life.

"Is it working yet?" I asked him. "Are you getting that X-ray vision?"

"Huh?" He gave me a startled look, making eye contact for a few seconds before refocusing on his goal.

"Looking for these?" I used both hands to pull down the top of my shirt. I gave him a full frontal blast of the peaches. "Here they are," I said. "Live and in person for one night only."

Mr. Jackson jerked his head up, looked at the ceiling, and slowly backed away. He said to my companion, while still looking at the ceiling, "Always nice to see you, Rhonda."

After he'd left, Rhonda said, "Gary and I used to date. Did I ever tell you that?"

"You and Mr. Jackson? I had no idea."

"It was a long time ago," she said. "He's okay, if you can get past him constantly ogling younger women." She took a sip of her scotch. "I didn't mind.

He's the sort of man who likes to look, and I figured what's the harm in that? At least he looks in real life, and not on the computer like some guys. That's unnatural."

"What ended things with you two?"

"I found myself another guy who only had eyes for me. It didn't last, either, but it was wonderful for a while." She looked me in the eyes. "Do you know what I mean? A guy who only sees you?"

"Sort of. It was like that with the actor."

She snorted. "Are we not saying his name anymore?"

"Fine. It was like that with Dalton Deangelo. Nisha and I went to this big fundraiser with him, and every time I looked over at him, he was staring back at me. There were a lot of girls in low-cut dresses there, and they were invisible to him."

Rhonda dipped a chicken wing in the blue cheese dip and pointed it at me like a magic wand. "Tell me again. Why did you dump him?"

"Because I was dating Adrian. The tall blond guy."

"I know who Adrian is. You've only been complaining about him to me for the last few months." She chewed on the chicken wing. "And where is Mr. Near-Genius-IQ right now?"

"Working at Ralph's Garage with Luca," I said. "He'll probably come by later and join us if we're still here in a bit. He does need to eat regularly. Are you okay to stick around for more than one drink? Someone's got to eat all this free food."

Rhonda said, "I'm already in trouble with my cat. What's a few more hours?"

I pulled out my phone. "I'll send Adrian a message and let him know we're over here."

"Tell him not to rush," Rhonda said. She pointed to a group of men over by the pool tables. "Look. I think you have some new fans."

One of the guys at the pool table held up a magazine—not Rhonda's, but a different one, with a different pose of me in my underwear—and pointed at me. He yelled across the bar, "Is this you?"

I gave him a noncommittal half-shrug.

That was all it took to get him, along with all eight of his friends, over to the bar where Rhonda and I were sitting.

Rhonda jumped into action, managing the crowd like a professional. She asked everyone their names and then got them to calm down and only ask me one question at a time.

Soon, I was signing my autograph on another magazine, then on T-shirts, then on bare chests.

The guys were all firefighters, with their own claim to fame on a fundraising calendar. We talked about photo shoots and even swapped modeling tips. Most of their tips were about dehydrating themselves to make their abdominal muscles show. I was glad I'd been hired for my other assets.

The drinks and platters of food kept coming, as did the fans.

For the next several hours, the crowd of men surrounding us never thinned. In fact, I had to pinkie-swear that I'd be right back just to get away to use the washroom.

In the ladies' room, a trio of women mobbed me, albeit more politely than the men. Word had been traveling around the pub, and everyone had been running up to Bookworm Books to buy magazines from Garnet.

The trio gushed about my gorgeous photos, and how I was an inspiration to all of them. They'd been wanting to talk to me for hours but hadn't been able to make it through the perimeter of guys.

I thanked the ladies and begged them to let me use the washroom first. "Give me a minute to do what I came in here for," I said. "As soon as I'm done, I'll pose for pictures with you." I looked around the washroom. "Not in here."

The women apologized and went to wait outside the ladies' room for me.

I was alone, but for how long? I went as quickly as I could.

While I was washing my hands, I heard people talking outside the bathroom door. The women were stopping someone else from coming in, citing that there was a famous model in the washroom who deserved some privacy.

I took a moment to look at myself in the mirror. I looked how I always looked, which wasn't *quite* good enough.

I opened my purse and applied an extra layer of makeup. Not because I was insecure, but because I'd learned from Mitchell that a woman's makeup had to be heavier so it looked right on camera.

Then I blew myself a kiss at my reflection and walked out to greet my adoring fans.

Chapter 10

It was raining, so even though the lineup for brunch at Delilah's was shorter than it had been during the summer, the bookstore was busier than ever. People crowded in to browse the books while taking a break from the rain.

Mid-morning, two girls in their late teens—one with dark hair and one with red hair—came to the counter to buy magazines.

My heart skipped a little. My photograph was in two of the magazines the girls were buying. I wondered what they would think when they opened the magazines and saw me in there.

They probably wouldn't recognize me as the young woman who'd sold them the magazine—who would think to check?—but they would have a reaction. Most people did. It was becoming more common for advertisements to feature plus-sized models such as myself, but it was still a novelty. Most of the time, girls like me were lumped into a group photo that screamed diversity. It was less common for a curvy model to be presented on her own, without any explanation or implied editorial.

While I rang up their purchases, the girls chatted with each other about boys. They were discussing what some guy's mysterious text messages might mean.

The dark-haired girl looked right at me and asked, "Do you have a boyfriend?"

"I do," I said.

She asked, "Does it get easier?"

Her friend giggled.

I replied, "In what way?"

She pulled out a pack of sugarless mint gum and offered me a piece after popping two in her mouth. "You know," she said vaguely. "Does it get easier to figure out what they want from you?"

"Oh, that's easy," I said. "They want *everything*, but only when it's convenient for them."

The red-haired girl said, "Told you so," to her friend.

The dark-haired girl asked me, "What about older guys? Like, if you date someone who's five years older than you?"

Her friend giggled again. They were talking about someone specific.

"I'm not sure about that," I answered. "My current boyfriend is my age."

"But that never works," the dark-haired girl said. "Girls are more mature than boys. If he's your age, then it's like dating someone younger than you."

"It is?"

Her friend said, "Don't listen to her. She's never had a boyfriend."

The other girl said, "Neither have you."

Both girls giggled.

"Whatever you do, don't rush into it," I said.

They both stopped giggling and stared at me like the old, boring person I had just revealed myself to be.

I popped the mint gum in my mouth and said, "Never mind my advice. Get out there and break some hearts, including your own. It's the only way to love."

"Uh, thanks," the dark-haired girl said sarcastically. "But who cares about love?"

The red-haired girl pouted and said, "I do."

They frowned at each other.

The dark-haired girl said to her friend, "That's the problem with you. Everything's about love with you, and it's all or nothing."

The redhead snorted. "That's my problem? I don't have a problem. Your problem is you don't even believe in love."

"What's love ever done for me?"

The redhead turned away from her friend and said to me, "I apologize for my friend. She's desperately in love with someone who doesn't know she exists."

"That's a tough one," I said.

The girls gathered their magazines, thanked me for my perspective then went on their way.

When they got outside, they ducked under a large umbrella being held by another girl who had been holding their place in the line for Delilah's.

The next person who came to see me at the counter was Carla, the white-haired woman who came in regularly to see Cujo. We'd gotten to know each other over the last few months, though she was pretty tight-lipped about her own life.

"Hi, Peaches," Carla said. "Were those girls who were just here asking you for your autograph?" Carla knew about my ad campaign. She'd been very supportive.

"They were just regular customers," I said. "Sometimes I wonder if they ever open the magazines, see the ads, and recognize me after the fact, even though I know that's pretty unlikely. I have kind of a generic face. I'm not like an actress, with one particular feature that stands out, like eyes that are a bit too wide apart."

"You have a lovely face," Carla said.

"So do you," I said.

The older woman touched her fingertips to her cheek delicately. "I did do some modeling back in my day. It was different then. We didn't have all the internet stuff. You could be everywhere there was to be, and still be nobody."

"Were you everywhere, Carla? I had no idea. You've been holding out on me."

"Mostly catalogs," she said. "But there was a time when every home got the catalogs regularly. I really was everywhere."

"You should bring some in! I'd love to see them sometime."

She smiled. "Maybe I will." She leaned forward and peered over the counter to see the true object of her admiration, the real reason she'd dropped by. Cujo. She asked, "Is he sleeping?"

"He was chasing some perps in his dreams earlier, but he's just dozing now." Dozing was what I called it when he had one eye partly open and was tracking my movements.

I invited Carla to come around the counter. We both bent down and patted the German shepherd until he fully woke up.

Cujo had been spending a lot of time at the bookstore that fall. Adrian was always busy working on different job sites, on various projects that were often messy and dirty. The dog was accustomed to being around people and didn't do well at home on his own, so I'd become his daytime babysitter. Cujo typically spent most of my shift snoozing under the counter. Most people didn't even notice. We had a sign on the front door warning people with allergies that a pet was on the premises, but it hadn't been an issue. People were used to seeing cats in bookstores. If anything, Cujo was an attraction. It turned out a lot of people had a special fondness for German shepherds.

Cujo got to his feet and gave Carla some sloppy kisses. He'd recovered nicely from the summertime bear attack, though he did have a slight limp that he played up sometimes to get extra treats and sympathy.

Carla asked, "Do you think he'd like to go for a walk?"

Cujo heard the W word—his hearing was excellent—and wagged his tail.

I handed Carla the leash. "Have fun out there. Bring him in through the back door when you're done. I've got a bunch of towels back there so we can get him dried off again."

Carla pulled up her waterproof hood and headed out with the dog.

The store had also cleared out, and I was suddenly completely alone.

I walked over to the magazine display. I opened a few magazines to my pictures and left them that way.

Ten minutes later, the front door jingled, and I rushed over to the magazines to close them again.

Chapter 11

My sixteen-year-old coworker, Garnet Langtree, arrived on time for his usual Saturday afternoon shift.

Cujo sensed Garnet's arrival immediately and greeted the dark-haired young man with a gruff bark.

Garnet barked back.

Cujo got excited, bouncing around like a puppy and barking some more.

Garnet ran circles around Cujo, also barking.

It was their routine, and the dog loved it.

Once they'd both calmed down, Garnet gave me a wide-eyed look and said simply, "There's another one."

"Another what?"

He looked around. Bookworm Books was empty at the moment. Someone had opened the door a moment earlier, then decided against browsing due to all the barking.

Garnet gave me a serious look and said, "Another half-sibling."

"Oh!" I'd almost forgotten about Garnet's search for relatives. The previous month, he'd made contact with a female half-sibling, but he'd been uncertain about meeting her in person.

"It's a guy this time," Garnet said. "He's older than me."

"Does that make it easier? You won't have to worry about liking him too much."

"I think it's going to be a lot easier. This one and the other girl already know each other."

"Lucky you," I said. "It's like a ready-made family."

"I don't know their names yet, but we're going to meet up." Garnet bounced from one foot to the other. "All three of us."

"What did your dad say about all this?"

"Nothing." Garnet waved both hands dramatically. "I'm not telling him anything until after I've met these people. My parents have been so weird about the whole thing. I just want to do this on my own."

"I hope it works out," I said. "It's brave of you to put yourself out there. I truly hope you get whatever you're looking for."

He continued bouncing on the balls of his feet. "I just want to find out the truth that's underneath everything."

"The truth underneath everything?" I gave him a wary look. "That sounds an awful lot like something Mr. Adrian Stromquist would say."

Garnet took off his jacket and scarf and tossed them under the counter, next to Cujo's dog bed. "I talk to Adrian sometimes. He's doing those custom closet organizers at my house right now. I was talking to him this morning before I came here. I told him everything. He's a good listener."

"You told Adrian all about the DNA stuff?"

"Yeah." Garnet frowned and ran his hands through his dark, silky hair. "Actually, he got a bit weird about it. He kept saying that my father—the one I don't know—shouldn't have been shut out of my life. He said it wasn't right, and that if my mom wouldn't tell me the whole truth underneath everything, I should sue her." His dark eyes bugged out. "Like, legally."

"Yes, Garnet. Legally is the only way to sue people." I leaned down and hugged Cujo to my leg. "I'm sure your mom has been trying to do what's best for you all along, even when it might not seem that way."

Garnet scowled. "Why do you always do that?"

"Do what?"

"Take her side. Is it a female thing?" His chest puffed up.

I held up both hands. "I'm on your side, dude. Trust me. I love your mom's music, because who doesn't, but I'm Team Garnet all the way."

"Oh." The wind died down in his sails.

"When are you meeting these two half-siblings of yours?"

"Today," he said.

"That's exciting. Where's the meeting? Somewhere public, I hope."

"They're coming here at closing time," he said. "Is that okay? I'll lock up, so nobody will walk in on us. I figured it might be better than meeting out in the open. In case it gets, you know..." He made a gagging face.

I had no idea what he meant. Could the meeting get uncomfortable to the point of someone vomiting? I supposed it could.

I asked, "Would you feel more comfortable if I was here?"

His eyes lit up. "You'd do that for me?"

"I think you knew I would, Garnet." I gave him a knowing look. "I think that's why you set up the meeting here."

He looked away and chewed on his lower lip. "I dunno." He scratched the back of his neck. "If you're not doing anything, I guess you could hang out for a bit."

"I'm an internationally famous curvy underwear model," I said, lifting my nose in the air. "There are memes about me all over the internet. Several body-positivity movements are simultaneously exalting me for being the right kind of fat, while criticizing me for being not nearly fat enough. I'm an extremely busy woman, Garnet Langtree, but I suppose I might pop back in around closing time today. Just to make sure these so-called half-siblings aren't planning to kidnap you."

He pulled his head back. "Why would anyone kidnap me?"

"For the ransom," I said. "You're rich."

"I'm not rich."

"No, but your grandma is, and so's your mom."

"Oh, right." He stuffed his hands in his pockets. "I bet my grandma already knows who my father is, and who all the others are. Lana Langtree knows *everything*."

"Probably." I ruffled his shiny dark hair. "But soon you'll know the truth, kiddo."

He gave me a shy smile, reminding me of a certain dark-haired actor. He was a sweet kid. I hoped he wasn't about to get his heart broken.

"It's about time," he said.

"I hope you're ready for whatever happens next," I said. "I happen to know someone who got into a world of trouble when he connected with some of his genetic relatives. His sister wanted to use him then extort him."

"Are you talking about Dirtbag McDribbles?"

Dirtbag McDribbles was one of Garnet's pet names for Dalton Deangelo. The previous summer, Dalton had dated Garnet's mom, and Garnet hadn't forgiven him for it.

"That is the person to whom I am referring," I said. "The funny thing is, I actually told him to do what you did, with the DNA thing. I didn't tell him who you were, of course. I just said you were a friend. But after that whole crazy rumor went around about him dating a relative, I thought he should get ahead of his family tree so he didn't end up accidentally dating someone who actually *was* his sister. That wouldn't be good for his anxiety."

Garnet gave me a blank stare. "Who cares? That guy is the worst."

A hilarious idea came to me. "You know what would be funny?"

"What?"

"Never mind," I said. I'd been about to suggest that Dalton could be Garnet's long-lost brother. Wouldn't that be something?

"What?"

"Forget it," I said. "It was a joke in very poor taste. I'll keep it to myself, since I bruise easily and you strike me as a shin kicker."

The front door jingled. The customer who'd been scared off by all the barking had rallied some courage and returned.

"Well, I should be on my way," I said, grabbing my purse.

Cujo wagged his tail as he looked at my purse, me, then Garnet. He paced the area, unsure what was expected of him. Was it really time to leave the bookstore? The dog liked me, but he *loved* Garnet.

"What?" I said to the dog. I'd become a person who talked to pets like they could understand me.

Cujo yawned.

Garnet said, "You're coming back later, right?" As he gave me a pleading look, Garnet looked much younger than his sixteen years.

"I'll come back ten minutes before closing. I have my phone, so call me if anything happens before I get here."

Garnet started playing with the dog's ears. "Can Cujo stay? He's good company."

"He is good company," I said. "Sure. I'll get him after I come back."

I gave the dog a pat goodbye, showed Garnet a few things I hadn't finished yet for the day, and went out the back door.

It was still raining.

I stopped under the overhang to button up my jacket.

The cook from Delilah's, Donny, was leaning on the wall next to the dumpster, protected from the rain by the building's overhang. He was shoveling food into his mouth from a bowl and greeted me with a friendly nod.

"Hey, Donny," I said. "How's life treating you?"

He lifted a blackened piece of food toward me and said, "Living the dream. How 'bout you?"

"Same."

"How's the modeling business?"

"A lot like the regular business, except for the one week a year when I do photoshoots."

"One week is a lot more than anyone wants of me in my underwear." He patted his midsection. "Hey, why is there no plus-sized movement for men? Who can regular guys like me look up to as a role model?"

"Comedians, I guess?"

Donny tilted his head to the side. "That works. Plus I am pretty funny."

"Glad I could help."

"By the way, my wife's a big fan," he said. "It's costing me a fortune in underwear. She has to buy everything with your name on it."

"Sorry about that."

He grinned. "That's okay. That's what money's for."

"I take it you're a fan, too?"

"Yeah!" He quickly added, "Of the underwear. I don't look at the pictures."

"Sure you don't." I winked at him and pulled out my phone to check messages.

Nisha was at work, and so was Adrian.

Adrian was no longer working for Gordon Olivier now that the liquor store was running smoothly. He had also finished Luca's renovation at the garage.

For the month of October, he would be helping some family friends with their custom carpentry business. He was currently at the Langtree residence —Garnet's house. I'd been there once before. The home, a gorgeous restoration, was within walking distance of Baker Street.

Since I would be needed at the bookstore again in a few hours to prevent any possible kidnappings, I didn't want to go all the way home and get too comfortable in my sweatpants. Once the sweatpants went on, it was hard to get them off.

I cracked open the back door and yelled to Garnet, "Would you and your family mind if I went over to your place to check out the new closets?"

Garnet replied, "Go for it."

I closed the door, said goodbye to Donny, and headed off to visit Adrian at his current work site.

Chapter 12

Adrian's new van was parked in front of the Langtree residence. He was definitely in there. I hadn't sent him a message because I wanted to surprise him. I'd brought some of the treats from Donut Joe's that he liked, plus a coffee.

I rang the doorbell, and Adrian answered. He was wearing a worn-out pair of jeans and one of his old Megasoystick T-shirts. His busy work schedule had caused him to lose a few pounds, so he looked more than ever like the young, skinny Adrian I'd known in high school, except for the scruffy beard and lack of lip ring.

"It's you," he said with surprise.

"Am I catching you at a bad time?"

"Not at all." He backed up and invited me into the house.

It was an enormous place, and gorgeous. I'd gushed about it on my first visit, when I'd been invited to Garnet's sixteenth birthday party.

We went up to the master bedroom, and he showed me what he was working on.

"This isn't a closet," I said. "It's an entire room."

"It's a closet if you say it is," he said.

"Rich people," I said with a head shake.

He took the coffee from my hands, took a sip, closed his eyes, and said, "You're the best."

I batted my eyelashes. "The best what?"

"The best everything," he said.

I pretended to kick him in the shin.

"The best girlfriend," he said, grinning.

"That's what I thought," I said. I looked around at all the gleaming shelves. "How are you enjoying this line of work?"

"It's not that exciting," Adrian said. "But it's good money, at least until the next thing comes along."

"And what will that be? You've already moved a bookstore, opened a liquor store, renovated a garage, and now you're doing high-end closets. What's next? Building a house from scratch with your bare hands? Running for mayor?"

He rubbed the blond scruff on his chin. "Mayor, huh? I like the sound of that."

"Don't bother," I said.

"You don't think I could win?"

"I'm sure you could, but then what would the city do in a month when you decided it was more appealing to be a lion tamer?"

He put his coffee on a furniture unit with drawers, set down the snacks I'd brought as well, and grinned as he put his arms around me. "You're the only lion I'm interested in taming."

"Meow," I replied.

"Meow," he said back.

"You seem happier than usual to see me."

He leaned down and kissed my neck. "I'm always happy to see you," he murmured. "I'm just bad at showing it."

"Like whenever other people are around," I said.

He kept kissing my neck. "Then it's a good thing there's nobody around right now."

"For now," I said.

"Peaches, I know I've been a bad boyfriend lately. I get too obsessed with work. But you've got my full attention right now." He nuzzled my ear. "Let me make it up to you."

"Now? You're at work."

"Since when has that ever stopped us?"

I pulled away. "Behave yourself. I only stopped by to say hello and check out the fancy closets. Is it just the one?"

"There's more." He took my hand and led me down the hall on a tour.

Since the separation and divorce of Dale Langtree and his famous singer wife, Jade, Dale had been redecorating the home he shared with his two children, Perry and Garnet. According to Garnet, Dale had been changing everything that had been Jade's choices. Every wall had been painted a new color—dove gray—and the light fixtures had been changed to sleek, modern versions finished in a retro brass. The gleaming brass looked like a million bucks next to all the pale gray.

The closets were nice, too. Some of them weren't even full rooms but actual closets.

"Nice work, Mr. Stromquist. You're quite the craftsman."

"They've had a lot of tradesmen coming and going," Adrian said. His icy-blue eyes lit up. "You have to see the new shower."

"I don't know if I have to..."

He led me into a tiled, fixtureless room that felt like a blank canvas.

"Where's the shower going in?" I asked. "That corner?"

"Close," Adrian said, his expression teasing. "Guess again."

I pointed to a different corner. "Over there?"

"Keep guessing."

There were only two corners left. One had a sturdy-looking, rustic wooden bench.

"That one."

"Nope."

I sighed. "Over there." I pointed to a tower of bathing products.

"Nope."

"You are so weird, Adrian Stromquist. Why'd you bring me in here?"

"For this." Adrian pressed some gleaming buttons on the wall. A mist began falling from the tiled ceiling. There was a gurgle, then steam came hissing out of the walls.

I let out a yelp and went for the door.

Adrian caught me with his long arm and held me tight. "You're already wet," he said. "Why not relax and enjoy it?"

"I'm not that wet yet."

A square hatch above me opened. A broad, steady stream of warm water came pouring down on my head.

"Now I'm wet," I said.

"We're both wet," he said.

"You can't do carpentry work when you're soaking wet," I said. The water continued pouring down on my head.

"I can put our clothes in the dryer," he said. "Everything you've got on is wash and wear, right?"

"Oh, Adrian. Since when did you think I was a dry-clean-only kind of girl?"

"We might as well get these off you," he said, helping me with my shirt.

The tiled room was filling up with steam. I backed away, allowing a cloud of steam to envelop me. I couldn't see anything, let alone my boyfriend. I could barely see my hand in front of my face.

Adrian laughed. "Where'd you go?"

I made a spooky ooOOoh sound. "I could be anywhere."

He swept his long arms around until he caught me. "Gotcha." He pulled me in and held me tight. "I'm not going to let you get away."

I giggled, then I turned toward him and kissed him as the warm water misted down.

He helped me out of my clothes, and I helped him out of his.

We eventually made our way over to the rustic bench and discovered that it was, indeed, as sturdy as it had appeared to be.

Chapter 13

I left the Langtree residence dressed in the freshly laundered version of the same clothes I'd left home that morning in.

The rain was still coming down, which disguised the fact that my shoes were still damp from my adventure in the walk-in steam room.

As I'd promised Garnet, I walked in through the back door of Bookworm Books at ten minutes before closing.

There were no customers in the store, which wasn't unusual for the end of the day on a Saturday.

Garnet was pacing nervously, doing laps around the central display shelves. Cujo was sleeping under the counter.

Garnet nodded at me and kept pacing.

"You're going to wear out the new floor," I said to him.

He finally stopped pacing and gave me a wide-eyed look. "What if they don't show up? They're not coming, are they? What if they walked by, took one look at me through the window, and decided not to come in?"

"Let's give them until the appointment time. Then, if nobody shows up, I promise to freak out with you."

The door jingled.

In walked Dalton Deangelo. I hadn't seen the handsome actor since the night of the fundraiser, over three months ago. His hair was different. It was shorter, but I knew that face. I remembered it well, plus I'd been watching him once a week in the new season of *One Vamp to Love*.

"Not now," I said to him, pointing at the door. "We're closed."

The actor who played Sir Drake Cheshire gave me a sheepish grin.

"You aren't closed," he said. "According to the sign, the store's still open for another ten minutes. I need to buy some books about, uh, kegel exercises."

"They'll still be here tomorrow," I said.

Garnet puffed up his chest and swaggered toward the handsome actor. "You heard the lady. You're not welcome here."

Dalton looked at Garnet, who had been growing that fall and was the same height as Dalton. Then he said, "Is that any way to greet your big brother?"

The door jingled, and another person walked in. Josie Ranger. Jocko Ranger's other daughter, and Dalton's half-sister. Also, by the look of things, Garnet's half-sister.

In hindsight, it would seem incredibly obvious—they were famous, which was why they'd wanted to see Garnet in person, rather than sharing their identity online like anyone else would have.

At the time, though, I was as shocked as a person could be.

There they were. Josie and Dalton. And Garnet. In the bookstore. All at the same time. Three offspring sired by the man who bragged about seducing women—including my own mother—in twenty minutes flat.

Garnet's mouth opened. A croaking sound came out.

Josie hissed at Dalton, "I told you to wait, you big dummy. It's not time yet. We're ten minutes early."

"I couldn't wait any longer," Dalton said.

Garnet started to sway.

Cujo, suddenly awake and alert, jumped out from behind the counter and started barking furiously at the newcomers.

Josie screamed, frightened by the dog.

Garnet was still swaying, and he wasn't talking.

Cujo became frantic and started nudging me forward, like he expected *me* to do something.

Garnet was really swaying. Cujo gave me one more nudge. I ran forward and caught Garnet mid-faint. The kid was heavier than he looked.

Cujo kept making noises—not barking, but not friendly, either.

Josie slipped out the door without a word. She stood on the other side of the glass, watching the scene from the safety of the street.

Cujo stalked forward, haunches up. He growled at Dalton and backed him all the way up into a corner.

Dalton held out both hands. "Easy, boy." He asked me, "Who's your friend?"

"That's Cujo. He's a retired police dog. Sometimes he gets the urge to serve and protect."

Dalton said, chuckling, "I'm not a bad guy, pooch. I swear."

"You're breathing," I said to Dalton.

"I am," he said.

"No panic attack," I said.

"It was always more about social anxiety," he said. "Dogs don't bother me much. Cujo's being a good boy. I know he's only trying to protect you."

Cujo stopped growling, sat down, and let his tongue hang out.

Dalton asked me, "How's the kid?"

I was slowly lowering Garnet to the floor. "Just stunned," I said. "Are you really his half-brother, or is this all some elaborate con?"

"Look at the kid," Dalton said. "Look at him, and you tell me."

The resemblance was definitely there, but part of me was still in denial.

"Lots of people have dark hair and dark eyes," I said.

Cujo barked at Dalton. It was his playful bark.

Dalton asked, "What's he saying? The dog?"

"He wants you to throw his ball around." I went to the counter and grabbed the slobber-coated tennis ball. I bounced it toward the front door. Cujo ignored it and continued staring at Dalton, who hadn't budged from his corner.

I looked down at Garnet, on the floor, then at Dalton.

"He does resemble you," I said. "Are you sure you guys are a match? Did you use a reputable website?"

Dalton said, "Come on. He's like a clone of Jocko. He looks more like my father than I do."

I jerked my head up and scanned the front windows. "Jocko's not here, is he?"

Dalton looked like he might laugh. "Of course not. That's the last thing this family needs."

"*This family*," I repeated. "I can't believe it. This is all so messed up. This means you dated your half-brother's mom, Jade."

Dalton lifted his chin. "Jade is not related to me in any way," he said. "It sounds bad when you describe our relationship that way, but she and I aren't connected, except for through my dad. And, as for that, I didn't know at the time. She didn't know I was his son, either. She didn't know who my dad was until Jocko came out with that crazy story about me and you."

"So she's known for a few months. Is that why she was giving Garnet the runaround?"

Dalton shrugged. "Jade figured that, given everyone's history, it might not be the right time to tell young Garnet. I had already sent my DNA to that company, like you suggested. When I got an email from Garnet, I called Jade and told her that he was old enough to know, and I'd tell him."

"You talked to Jade about all this?"

He nodded.

"Why isn't she here?" I asked. "She should be here."

"She's in LA, filming for the singing show. She's contractually obligated to be there. I'm sure if her schedule wasn't so tough, she'd be here."

Garnet moaned at my feet. He was starting to revive.

"I'm not so sure about her story," I said. "But that's her business."

Cujo let out an aggressive sneeze in the actor's direction, then turned and came over to lick Garnet's face.

Dalton took a tentative step out of the corner. He was still breathing normally. He seemed downright calm, considering the situation.

Josie opened the door a crack. "Is it safe to come in?"

"The dog is friendly," Dalton said. "Grab that tennis ball, and he'll probably be your new best friend."

She stayed outside the door and looked at me specifically. "You're not going to punch me any new freckles, are you?"

"Not unless you swing first," I said. "Get in here, Josie. Twist the bolt on the door behind you. The last thing we need right now is more people in here."

I knelt by Garnet and lifted his head into my lap.

Garnet's eyes opened. His face was wet from Cujo's tongue.

Garnet whispered, "Peaches? Did I pee my pants?"

I looked down. His jeans were the regular color. "You did not," I said.

He asked, "Are they still here?"

"They are both still here," I said. "Do you want them to leave?"

Garnet thought about it a minute, then rolled to his side and jumped up.

Cujo ran for his tennis ball and dropped it on Garnet's foot.

I put a hand on Garnet's shoulder. "Are you okay, kiddo?"

"Terrific," he said. He was wobbly on his feet.

"Right this way, sailor," I said, leading him over to a kid-sized chair in the corner, next to the picture books. He took a seat. The tall teenager looked very large on the undersized chair.

Josie was wringing her hands nervously. She looked smaller than I remembered. Everyone looked smaller when they didn't have a garden hose, or a camera.

I called Cujo to my side and started walking toward the back door.

"I'm just going to take the dog to his owner," I said. "That should give you three some time to get acquainted with each other."

Dalton gave me a worried look. "You'll come back, though, right?"

Garnet gave me a similar worried look—they really did resemble each other—and said, "Please come back, Peaches."

Josie didn't say anything.

"I'll be back... in about an hour," I said. "Can you three handle that?"

They all nodded.

I took Cujo with me and exited through the back door.

It had stopped raining during the short time I'd been inside the bookstore. What a difference a few minutes made. The air was chilly, but the sky was clearing rapidly. The shadows in the alley were long and dark from the thin autumn sun.

Donny, the cook from Delilah's, was in the alley again, eating a different meal of blackened food. He nodded at me and Cujo and said, "Living the dream."

Chapter 14

I phoned Adrian and asked him to come and meet me at the dog park to pick up Cujo.

The German shepherd was sniffing some smaller dogs when Adrian rolled up in his new van and whistled at us.

I waved hello.

Adrian leaned out the window and called out, "Hey, aren't you that famous underwear model from all the billboards? Is that you, Peaches Monroe? Can I have your autograph?"

"I'll sign your butt right now if you have one of those black felt pens that doesn't wash off."

He chuckled. "Don't tempt me."

I came over to the van and opened the sliding passenger door for the dog. Cujo put his front paws in and waited for me to give him a boost. The dog could jump a full-grown person running in the woods, yet he had issues hopping up into the new van. I leaned over and performed the dog-butt-lift. He wasn't the lightest dog in the world, but I was getting used to the maneuver.

"Thanks for coming to get him," I said to Adrian.

"Just him? I drove over here for my two-for-one deal."

"I can't hang out tonight."

"But I'm done with work."

"I didn't want to get into it on the phone, but you know how Garnet was planning to meet up with his mysterious half-siblings?"

"He may have mentioned it," Adrian said cagily.

"I know he told you," I said. "Anyway, they showed up at the store at closing time. Cujo was barking and making the girl nervous, which is why I had to take him away."

"Cujo barked at them? He's a pretty good judge of character. That could be a sign."

"Cujo also attacked me in the woods. He's not as smart as you think he is."

Adrian didn't say anything.

"Garnet's going to be okay, once they get over the awkwardness, but I promised I'd head back to the store to check in on him."

"That's nice of you. I'll come, too. He's a good kid. Cujo can nap in the van."

"No need," I said quickly. "It's, uh, already crowded enough as it is."

He gave me a hurt look. "You don't want me there? Wait. Are you punishing me for something?"

"It's nothing like that, I assure you. Can we talk about this tomorrow?"

He rubbed his scruffy chin. He was still in the driver's seat, and I was standing outside of the van, by the sliding door. With the way the dome light was lighting his face, it was hard for me to see his expression.

"I'll be pretty busy with work tomorrow," he said.

"It's Sunday. I thought we agreed you'd take Sundays off."

"I don't think so."

"Adrian, I distinctly remember having a discussion about Sundays."

He shook his head slowly. "Was it one of the discussions you have where you argue with the Adrian who lives inside your head? It must have been, because I don't remember talking about Sundays."

I sighed. He was probably right. I did argue with him in my head.

Adrian said, "You know what? I will take tomorrow off." He drummed the steering wheel.

"Let's do something fun. We can go to that trashy pancake place with the chocolate fountain. Then we can go hang out at the Pier. The tourists should be mostly gone by now."

"Are you sure? You're not going to call me tomorrow morning and cancel?"

"I've got it all figured out. I'll head over to the hardware store first thing in the morning, pick up the supplies, drop them off at the Langtree house, then swing by your place and pick you up. I'll have a good appetite worked up by then. Tell Nisha she's invited, too. My treat."

"Sounds great." I stepped back and started to close the door.

"Hang on," he said. "Not so fast. Did you say you met the half-siblings?"

Reluctantly, I answered, "Briefly."

"And? What are they like?"

I played with the handle for the door, making it squeak. My heart was heavy. My heart knew that I should have told him who they were, especially that one of the half-siblings was Dalton Deangelo. But then Adrian would know I was bailing on him to go see Dalton. Or, worse, he'd insist on coming with me, and his addition to the group dynamic would make the earlier disaster seem like a simple appetizer.

"They're eclectic," I said. "I promise to tell you everything tomorrow."

Adrian yawned. "Okay."

Cujo yawned and smacked his lips.

"Get some sleep," I told them both as I closed the door.

As the van drove away, I stood on the sidewalk next to the dog park, watching the red taillights disappear. The sun was setting. The rain had stopped, but the air was moist. The autumn air was going from invigorating to downright cold.

I turned and started walking back to the bookstore. My shoes were still damp from my adventures in the walk-in shower, and my toes were cold.

I picked up my pace, hurrying back.

Chapter 15

When I opened the back door to the bookstore, the first thing I heard was laughter.

The anticipatory dread that I'd been feeling dropped away. My shoulders returned to their regular position.

I walked in and found the three half-siblings relaxing on the tiny chairs and beanbags in the children's section. It was the most private part of the store, the one area that was shielded from the front windows by shelving.

They went quiet when they saw me.

Then, all at once, they all burst into laughter.

I tucked my hands into my jacket pockets and said, "This reminds me of a recurring nightmare I have."

That made them laugh even harder.

Garnet looked up at me from his beanbag and said, "They were telling me about the time you guys sprayed each other with the garden hose."

"We didn't spray *each other*," I said. "Dalton sprayed Josie, then she blasted me." I narrowed my eyes at the petite, short-haired young woman. "Since when do you two get along, anyways?"

Josie answered, "Since we decided to unite against a common enemy." She wrinkled her nose. "Our crazy father."

"And all of Los Angeles," Dalton said.

Then all of them laughed again, even Garnet, whose beef with Los Angeles had more to do with his mother's career than his own.

"Well, it seems like everything's under control here," I said. "I'll just head home and let you three continue to catch up."

"Don't go," Josie said, suddenly looking sad. "Peaches, you and I met under lousy circumstances. That wasn't the real me. I feel awful about everything that happened between us. I am truly very sorry." She got to her feet and walked toward me. Her lower lip trembled. "Part of my recovery is making amends, and I get that now. Finally." She held out her hand. "Can we start over?"

I took her small hand in mine and shook it. "We can't start over, because that's not possible. But I do accept your apology for spraying me with my own garden hose, stalking me with your camera, brokering the sale of those security drone photos of me running through the woods in my underwear, and whatever else you did that I don't know about."

She winced. "That's most of it," she said. "I may have posted some mean things about you on social media."

"Who didn't? Every time I'm on the internet in my underwear, it brings on a fresh onslaught of the worst human behavior."

She continued to hold my hand as she forced a smile. "That's fame for you. B-Listers like us get the worst trashing, and without the huge paychecks of the A-Listers."

I pulled my hand away from hers. "Who are you calling a B-Lister?"

Dalton piped up from his undersized kids' chair, "I'm a B-Lister, too. Our father, the action movie star, is the A-Lister."

Garnet waved his hand. "I'm a No-Lister."

"Don't say that," Dalton said. "A good-looking kid like you? Give me two months to get you into a boy band, or dating someone famous, and you'd be surprised. With that face, you could be a real heartbreaker."

Josie rolled her eyes. "Don't inflate his ego," she said. "He already looks like a miniature Jocko. We don't want our little brother turning into another monster."

Dalton said to Garnet, "Don't listen to her. Jocko has his flaws, but he's not a monster. Josie's only saying that because she had her allowance cut off."

Garnet asked, "How much was the allowance?"

The two older siblings exchanged a look. Dalton said, grinning, "You don't want to know."

Then all three of them laughed in unison.

I checked the time on my phone. There was a message from Adrian, asking how the family reunion was going. He also sent a photo of his three-legged rat, Munchies, enjoying a chicken-and-grape salad.

Josie returned to her seat, and Dalton waved for me to come join them. "Sit with us," he said.

The only remaining seat was right next to him.

"I should get home. This is my workplace, after all, and I did spend most of the day here."

Garnet jumped up, ran over to the control panel, and dimmed the store's lights. It was suddenly very cozy, like a private library.

"How about now?" Garnet asked. He explained to the others, "She loves hanging out inside the store after closing."

Josie looked around. "I can see why. It's even nicer with the lights dimmed."

"Come and relax with us," Dalton said, patting the little chair next to him. "Bernard is coming by shortly with some takeout food from a Malaysian place."

Garnet asked, "Who's Bernard? That's not another brother, is it?"

Josie giggled as she said, "That's his butler. Dalton has a butler."

Garnet's eyes bugged out. "That's so cool. You're like Batman."

"I *am* cool," Dalton said to Josie, sticking his tongue out.

Then all three of them were sticking their tongues out, comparing tongue length and seeing who could roll their tongues. All three could.

I sent a quick text update to Adrian, letting him know I'd be staying late but that everything was going well.

Then I took a seat in the tiny chair next to Dalton.

The actor put his arm around me, hugged me to his side in a friendly gesture, then dropped the arm away.

The three continued talking and teasing each other. Eventually, they let me in on some of their jokes.

Bernard showed up with the Malaysian takeout food, and we enjoyed a feast inside the bookstore, sitting cross-legged on the floor and using the children's reading table.

The siblings kept talking about how their father would have loved to have been there... and ruined everything for them.

Little did they know, many miles away, Jocko Ranger would soon be receiving word about the family reunion.

The action movie star would arrive in town four weeks later, with some surprises of his own.

Chapter 16

The teen girls who'd bought magazines the previous month came back to Bookworm Books.

The dark-haired girl pulled a magazine from her backpack, opened it to the picture of me in sparkly underwear, and asked, "Is this you?"

Her red-haired friend, who looked mortified, said, "I'm sorry. She's been obsessed."

I pretended to study the magazine page. "It sure looks like me," I said, playing it cool. "I don't think I have an identical twin, so it must be me."

"I knew it," the dark-haired girl said. "Told you so," she said to her friend, sticking out her tongue.

The redhead girl's jaw dropped.

I grabbed a metallic-ink pen. "Want me to autograph it for you?"

The dark-haired girl handed over the magazine. "Yes, please!"

"Always nice to meet a fan," I said. "When you tell the internet about this, which I'm sure you will, please let the internet know I'm charismatic in person, and even better looking."

The redhead said, "I wish I had your butt."

"I get that a lot," I said. "I'd offer a squeeze, but my boyfriend doesn't like that."

The redhead went back to looking mortified.

I signed the magazine.

The dark-haired girl asked, "What do you think of the new season of *One Vamp to Love*? Honestly?"

"It's the best season yet," I said.

She frowned. "You're only saying that because you work for the studio."

"That's true," I said. "I go to a weekly hypnotism session where they program me to say whatever the week's main talking points are. This season of *One Vamp to Love* is the best season ever! I enjoy it so much that I watch it live when it airs, and I sit through all the commercials, paying very close attention to the messages from the show's sponsors. That's what a true fan does."

She kept frowning. "Really?"

"I'm also contractually obligated to eat three donuts per week to maintain my figure."

"Really?" Her eyebrows went up. She believed me.

"It's a dream job," I said. "I am literally living the dream."

"Cool," she said, then the two girls left, giggling happily.

That was when my best friend and roommate, who'd been sitting on a chair nearby, reading the last pages of novels, chortled to herself.

I walked over to Nisha and yanked another ruined novel from her hands. "Do I amuse you, ma'am?"

"You do," she said. "I thought the studio didn't like it when you messed with people."

"They don't," I said. "That's why I'm not allowed to do any of my own social media stuff. They have a team that writes better content than anything I could come up with."

"I'm not so sure about that. You are pretty creative."

"Creative, yes. But I'm also NSFW. That means Not Safe for Work."

"I know what NSFW means." She reached for another novel and flipped to the back page. "Well, that's tragic," she said, and replaced the book on the shelf.

The front door jingled.

Garnet Langtree arrived for his shift. He was wearing sunglasses, even though the weather was gray.

Nisha whistled and said, "Look at you, Mr. Hollywood."

Garnet whipped off the glasses and grinned. "My brother got them for me. He sent a whole case."

Nisha said, "Sounds like you two are getting along. How do you like having a famous half-brother?" Garnet had told Nisha about his meeting with Dalton Deangelo and Josie Ranger the month before. Garnet's family and a few other friends knew, but the press hadn't gotten wind of it yet—nor had Jocko Ranger, as far as we knew.

"I like the free swag," Garnet said. "And Dalton's okay. Josie is annoying, just like my other sister, but she's okay, too."

Nisha replied, "Now all you need to do is meet Jocko. Then everything will be in alignment, as it should be. Your life will leap forward after that happens."

"My life will leap forward? You mean I'll finally get a girlfriend?"

"If that's what's meant to be," Nisha said.

"I don't get it," Garnet said. "Why do I have to make an effort to do anything, if everything is already preordained?"

I ruffled his dark hair. "Look at you," I said. "Using big words like *preordained*. It's a good question, though. What do you say, Nisha?"

"There are many forks on a person's path," Nisha said, not at all stumped. "The future *is* set out for you, but there are many versions. Many futures."

Garnet wrinkled his nose. "You mean multiple universes?"

"Not exactly," Nisha said. "The paths all go to the same place, in the end."

"So, converging universes."

"Maybe," she said.

The phone rang, so I left those two to their philosophical conversation.

I answered with a cheery "Good afternoon, Bookworm Books. All our titles come with genuine book smell."

A male voice replied, "What?"

"You've reached Bookworm Books. We don't have any bookworms, thanks to regular cleaning, but we do offer a free bookmark with every purchase."

"Right," the male voice said. "Is someone named Garnet working there today?"

"He certainly is. Would you like to speak with him, or is there something I can help you with?"

"Who is this?"

"This is Peaches."

There was a pause, and his voice got deeper. "Veronica's daughter?"

"Yes," I said slowly.

"You sound like her," the man said. "Your mother is a fine woman."

"She certainly is. What can I help you with today?"

"How late are you open?"

"I'm not going to lie to you, sir. We are open until six. But that doesn't mean you can rush in here at five minutes to six and then hang out for half an hour. Normally, I'd tell people on the phone that we close at five-thirty, just to prevent such behavior. But, since you know my mother, I'm giving you the straight goods."

"The straight goods," he repeated, sounding amused. "What if I come in before five?"

"You're welcome to come in at five. Garnet can help you if you have any questions."

"What about you?"

"I'll be at home, stress-testing a new pair of sweatpants."

"What would it take to get you to stick around a little longer? I haven't landed in the city yet, but I'd love to lay my eyes on Veronica's daughter in person."

"I could be convinced to stick around a bit longer," I said cagily. "It might help if you told me your name so I could run it against the stalker database."

"Jocko," he said. "Jocko Ranger."

I dropped the phone.

Chapter 17

Garnet took the news about Jocko Ranger's impending visit well.

And by *well*, I mean he did *not* faint or lose control of his bladder. He did, however, freak out.

An hour later, Garnet was so discombobulated and distracted that I told him to go home and get himself calmed down before he came back in time for the meeting with Jocko Ranger, the man who'd provided half his genetic material.

"I'm not coming back," Garnet said with a defiant snort. "That man can't ambush me at work. It's not fair."

"But Dalton and Josie met you here at the store."

"I agreed to that," he said. "This is different. I never gave that man my consent."

"I didn't give him mine, either. He has a history with my mother, and he was a bit creepy on the phone. Why should I have to be here if you aren't?"

Garnet patted me on the shoulder. "Because you're the manager of this place, Peaches. This is why Mr. Olivier pays you the big bucks."

"Big bucks? I barely make more than you," I said.

"But you have business cards with your name on them," he said, backing away. "Tell Jocko I said hi, and I'll have my people get in touch with his people." Then he sailed out the door.

Nisha, who had stuck around to see how things played out, gave me a wide-eyed look. "It's like a soap opera around here," she said. "Nothing this good happens over at Bumblebee, and we sell booze. It's not remotely fair. I wish we had a good scandal unfolding."

"Careful what you wish for," I said.

"What time is Jocko Ranger coming here?"

"He mentioned something about five o'clock." I checked the time. "Four hours from now."

Nisha wrinkled her nose. "I'll be at work. Maybe you can call someone else to be here with you for support. You can try Sunshine, or Brittany. They claim to have forgiven you for stealing Adrian from them. I bet either one of them would be happy to chaperone you and draw the heat from Jocko." She waggled her eyebrows. "Or both of them. They don't mind sharing, apparently."

"What makes you think I need a chaperone?"

"The fact that Jocko Ranger seduces women in twenty minutes flat."

"Sure, but he's my boyfriend's father," I said.

Nisha's head jerked. "Your *what*?"

"I mean he's my ex's father. He's Dalton's father. That's what I meant to say. And he's Garnet's father, for that matter. He's a *dad*. Plus he's so old. I would never be seduced by him."

Nisha crossed her arms.

"Plus he's crazy," I said. "He thought Dalton and I were involved in some sort of scheme that revolved around him. What a narcissist!"

"You're excited about meeting him. Your cheeks are flushed."

I patted my cheeks. They did feel warm. "I've got good blood flow to my face. It's the secret to my clear skin. I'm not flushed with excitement over Jocko Ranger showing up. I'm not my mother."

She gave me a knowing look. "You are *so* excited about meeting Jocko Ranger." She glanced around the bookstore. "Where do you think the seduction will happen? Right on the counter?"

"Nisha!"

She pointed to the kids' area. "How about over there, on the beanbag chairs?"

I narrowed my eyes at Nisha. "Stop projecting your twisted little fantasies onto me, Ms. Patel."

"What will Adrian think?" She made a tsk-tsk sound. "He will not be pleased when he finds out about this after the fact. He's still being passive-aggressive about the whole thing with Dalton and Josie."

I snorted. "Did you pick up on that? But how could that be? Adrian is so *subtle* about his feelings toward Dalton."

We both laughed. Adrian had been upset that I hadn't told him about my meeting with Dalton and Josie the month before until after it had happened. He only brought it up... constantly.

"We shouldn't make fun of Adrian," Nisha said. "He's only insecure because he knows he can't compete with Dalton."

"That's silly. He doesn't have to compete. I already chose him."

"Did you?"

I shrugged. "I'm with him."

"But Dalton isn't entirely out of your life. He could have been, but then it turned out he's related to your coworker. That means something. The universe is sending you a message."

"This universe, or a parallel one?"

She shook her head. "There's a reason Dalton is still swimming in your waters."

"Now you're just being weird. Swimming in my waters?"

"He's around," she said. "There are ripples."

I thought about it for a minute. There *were* ripples from Dalton being around. Whenever his name was mentioned, Adrian had a strong reaction. Sometimes I benefited from that reaction. Adrian had a jealous streak. Whenever I got attention from other men, it made him step up his game.

"You *like* having Dalton making ripples in your life," Nisha said. "Admit it."

"It's not the worst situation," I said. "I can use his ripples as a force for good. It's like how my mother gets my dad to hit the gym by mentioning that a new Jocko Ranger movie is coming out. The nice thing about Adrian being jealous of Dalton is I always have a date the night *One Vamp to Love* is airing, so I rarely get to watch it live with commercials, despite what I tell people."

Nisha gave me a long look, her dark-brown eyes missing nothing. "You two are an interesting couple. You bicker like a couple of old folks, but not always. When you're in the bedroom with the door closed, the bickering stops. Then you're like a couple of zoo animals."

I crossed my arms to match her posture. "Which ones? Which zoo animals?"

"Hyenas. Because of the laughter."

"Those high-pitched shrieks are Adrian's," I said. "He's very ticklish."

Nisha held up one hand. "Some things, I'd rather not know." She picked up her purse and pulled it onto her shoulder. "I should be getting over to the scandal-free booze shop."

"You guys aren't exactly scandal free. There's still the unsolved mystery of the disappearing strawberry yogurt."

Nisha shook her head. "Not anymore. Someone kept moving them into the crisper drawer. I found a dozen in there yesterday." She headed toward the door. "Call me if you need anything. I can get away if it's an emergency."

"I'll be fine," I said. "Jocko Ranger is just a person. And besides, maybe he's nervous about meeting me."

"He should be nervous," Nisha said. "You're trouble."

"Me?"

"You shook up Jocko's son's life every bit as much as Dalton shook up yours. And now you're shaking up Jocko's, too."

"I never did anything to Jocko. You sound as crazy as him."

"Think about it, Peaches. The ripples come from you. Thanks to your encouragement, telling Dalton to send in his DNA, three of Jocko's kids got together to conspire against him." She waved her finger at me. "You did this."

"I didn't mean to. I'm just a pebble in the lake. I didn't mean to make ripples. It was the universe that tossed me in."

"Sure." She gave me a head-to-toe scan. "If we want to avoid a twenty-minute seduction by Jocko, at least do something about how you look."

I looked down at myself. "What's wrong with how I look?" I was wearing a wrap dress that clung to my curves. My hair was down, and my makeup was perfect.

"You look like a model," Nisha said.

"I am a model."

"But you shouldn't look like one," she said. "Jocko's going to fall in love with you at first sight."

"That's the last thing I need. My mother would be so jealous."

"She would be. She's already struggling with getting older. It's the last thing she needs."

"What should I do?" I gathered my hair and pulled it up, fastening it with a loose knot. "Put my hair in a ponytail?"

Nisha looked at me a moment then sighed. "There's no point. You look gorgeous no matter what you do."

"I really do." I grabbed the pair of reading glasses we kept at the counter for people who'd forgotten theirs at home and needed them to sample books. I put on the glasses. "How about now?"

"You keep getting hotter. Now you look like the sexy librarian in a dirty movie."

I whipped off the glasses and shook out my hair.

"Show-off," Nisha said, grinning. "Good luck with Jocko. Don't do anything I wouldn't do."

She winked and left me to the bookstore.

Chapter 18

Jocko Ranger didn't arrive at five o'clock.

He phoned to say his plane was running behind—something about the wind—and said he'd come by at six o'clock, right when we closed.

This allowed me an additional hour to be nervous.

At five-thirty, I adjusted the lighting inside the store so that the interior was as bright as possible. I also changed the angle of the shelf by the kids' section so that every part of the store could be seen from the sidewalk.

There was no way I would allow myself to be talked into anything unseemly by Mr. Jocko Ranger. I wasn't moving furniture out of any kind of genuine fear of seduction. Or so I told myself. Moving stuff around helped calm my nerves. That was all.

At precisely six o'clock, the man I'd seen on the big screen countless times walked in the front door.

Jocko Ranger was in his early sixties, with a few lines on his handsome, rugged face. His hair was, as it had always been, jet black. His eyes were green, like Dalton's. He was clean-shaven, and looked exactly as he did in his action movies—at least in the early scenes, before everything devolved into chaos and action.

"Veronica's daughter," he said, smiling confidently as he approached me. "You are the spitting image of your beautiful mother."

He held out his hand. I shook it.

My whole body was numb. No matter how many times I'd told myself Jocko Ranger was just a man, I hadn't been prepared for meeting the superstar. He was a legend. An icon. He was Jocko Ranger.

He gave me a knowing look. "Cat got your tongue?"

"Never," I said. "It's nice to meet you."

"Same to you."

"How was your flight?"

"Long," he said. "I had a few connecting flights, and that's always tiring."

"You don't look tired," I said. He did not. He was a few inches shorter than he'd been inside my head, but I kept that to myself. He looked a lot like Dalton, except instead of a perfect nose, he had one that had been broken and healed crooked.

"Thanks," he said. "And thank you for not saying I'm shorter than you expected. I hate it when people say that."

"Tell me about it," I said. "When I meet people who've seen my photos, they always tell me I must have lost weight recently because I'm not as fat as they thought I was."

"Fat?" He still had my hand in his as he looked me over. "You're perfect," he said. "Don't listen to what anyone else says about your size or shape or anything else for that matter. *They* have a way of making you disappear, one piece at a time. *They* told me to fix this." He pointed to the dent on the bridge of his nose. "But who would I be without this dent on my nose? Not Jocko Ranger. I would be someone else. Someone not as famous as Jocko."

I pulled my hand away. "Do you always refer to yourself in the third person?"

"Yes," he said. "It's part of my... ego condition."

I bit my lip. "Oh?"

"I am aware of my ego condition, and my other shortcomings. These are things I am working on. Once I become the master of my ego, I plan to write a book to help others with theirs." He looked around at the books surrounding us. "There sure are a lot of books in here. Wow. I hope to immortalize myself in places like this one." He gave me a winning grin. "And I plan to help others. Of course."

I nodded. "You're not as nutty as I thought you would be."

"Thank you." He glanced over my shoulder, scanning the store. "Do you think my youngest will be returning to greet his dear ol' dad?"

I'd already told Jocko, when he'd called about running late, that Garnet wouldn't be there.

"He's digging in his heels," I said. "Honestly, I think he's waiting to get the report from me about whether or not you're the Big Bad Wolf."

Jocko bared his upper teeth in a wolfish grin. "How am I doing so far?" He snapped his teeth at me, pretending to want to bite.

I didn't flinch.

"You don't scare me," I said.

"Good. Where would you like to take me for dinner?" He rubbed his stomach. "I'm so famished, I might eat carbohydrates."

"I'm taking *you* out?"

"I don't carry a wallet," he said. "If you don't feed me soon, I may bite."

"We wouldn't want that," I said. "If you want something right away, I suppose we could go to Niro's. It's up the street. We can have dinner there. My treat."

He grinned and pulled a wallet from his leather jacket. "Just kidding about the wallet. You passed the test. Dinner is on me."

"Good one." I started flicking off lights to close the shop.

Jocko asked, "How long does it take you to shut things down?"

"About five minutes," I said. "I have to run a report on the computer. Why do you ask? Were you planning to seduce me in twenty minutes flat, like you do everyone else?"

"My new time to beat is fifteen minutes," he said. "But I would never do that to you, Peaches."

"Why not? Am I not cute enough?" I picked up my water cup and took a sip.

"You're my future daughter-in-law," he said.

I spat out the water in a spray. "I'm your *what*?"

"Come on," he said. "You've been with Dalton. You know what he's like. You two are a perfect match. I knew it the minute I saw your pictures."

"No, you didn't. You thought we were related. You went to that press with that crazy story. Poor Dalton had a complete meltdown about it."

"I was mistaken," Jocko said simply. "Now I understand that I was responding to something else that I detected—a match that was meant to be."

"Have you been talking to my roommate? She's obsessed with fate, and how there's no such thing as coincidence. She's always saying the universe wants things a certain way."

"But the universe does want things a certain way," he said. "The universe tried once, with me and your mother, but I was too foolish to make the leap. Now, the second time around, there's a second chance. I will not be so foolish."

"Are you talking about my mom? You'd better not be. She's happily married to a man I call Dad."

"That ship has sailed," Jocko said. "The second chance is you and Dalton. I haven't been a good father to him, but I'd like to make up for it now."

I stared at him, almost too stunned for words. "I'm not a gift you can give your son," I said. "I'm not a bargaining chip, or a karma point, or whatever it is you think I am."

"Oh, please," Jocko said, grinning confidently. "We both know that you two are meant to be. I've never seen my son as happy as he is when he talks about you. He had a wonderful time with you last month. He said you two talked for hours."

"We did," I said. Dalton and I had gone for a walk the night he met with Josie and Garnet. It was a detail I hadn't told Adrian or Nisha.

"He said you were unhappy with some aspects of your life," Jocko said.

"Who isn't? We talked about our problems. That's what friends do."

"It's also what lovers do," Jocko said.

"Dalton and I are just friends," I said.

"Why?"

"Because," I said. "Because that's how I want it to be."

"We shall discuss this further over dinner."

I wiped up the water I'd spit on the counter. It took me a minute to figure out what I'd been doing before Jocko had gotten me so agitated. I remembered and clicked the button to run the computer report.

While I did the closing procedures, Jocko browsed the memoir section. It was dim, lit only by the fixtures we left on overnight. He held the books at a distance, the way my father had been holding menus for the past couple of years. It was cute, seeing everyone's favorite action movie hero struggling with age-related vision problems.

I finished the closing-up procedures, surreptitiously sent Nisha a text update, then announced I was ready to go.

After we'd stepped outside and I'd locked the door, Jocko Ranger offered me his elbow in a very sweet and respectful gesture, like the kind a man might use around his future daughter-in-law.

Chapter 19

Jocko Ranger was, to my surprise, not a monster. He was dramatic, and he did shamelessly flirt with all the waitresses at Niro's, but he was also politely charming.

After the waitress cleared away our dinner plates, the conversation turned back to his plans to write a memoir.

He asked me, "What sort of customer buys a memoir by a celebrity?"

"Generally, it's women over forty," I said. "Sometimes it skews younger or male if it's a legendary rock star, or a male entrepreneur."

Jocko grinned. "I do appreciate a woman over forty. No offense to you, of course."

"None taken," I said.

He replied, "I'm sure the younger version of me would have found you very appealing."

"The younger version of you *did* find me appealing," I said. "First, there was you, seducing my mom, and then there was Dalton, with me."

He tipped his head back and let out a bellow of a laugh. The few diners in Niro's that hadn't yet realized Jocko Ranger was seated in the dining room finally took notice of him. People took photos of us and filmed us with their phones.

Jocko wiped a tear from the corner of his eye and said, "You really tell it like it is, don't you, Peaches Monroe?"

"If I didn't speak the truth, I wouldn't have anything to say."

His expression grew serious. He pulled a notepad from his pocket and made a note.

"That's a good line," he said, pointing at me with his pen. "Do I have your permission to put it in my memoir when I write about this dinner? Verbatim?"

"Sure," I said. "Can I ask you a personal question?"

His emerald-green eyes twinkled. "Those are my favorite questions. It's the giant ego I have. My favorite topic is me, me, me."

"Why does your daughter, Josie, have such a low opinion of you?"

"That's easy," he said. "She grew up with me. I was a terrible father more often than not. I was a lousy husband, too. I ignored her mother, and her mother took it out on Josie."

I leaned in. "And you just admit that? Over a casual dinner with someone you don't even know? While people are filming us on their cell phones?"

He nodded. "Of course I admit what I am."

"That's brave."

He shrugged. "If you're being chased by a bear, then you should keep running. If you're being chased by your mistakes, then you must turn around and face them." His dark eyebrows shot up. He pointed at the air with his pen. "Hang on. That's good, too." He wrote a few more lines in his notebook then said, "I may have found my unifying theme, thanks to you. I'll call it *facing the bear*."

"I saw a bear this summer," I said.

"You did?" He set down the pen and left the notepad on the table. "You'll have to tell me all about it over dessert."

The waitress returned, and Jocko requested their three most popular desserts.

After the waitress left, he said, "Always order an odd number of any course. That way your date is obligated to share dishes with you. Everyone knows sharing food creates intimacy and makes for a wonderful evening.”

“Is that tip going to be in your memoir?”

“Of course.” He smiled. “Now tell me about this bear you saw. Was it when Dalton took you trespassing to those hot springs?”

“We only saw a deer and a fawn that time,” I said. “I saw the bear when I was hiking with my boyfriend, Adrian, and his dog, Cujo.”

The trio of desserts arrived.

While we shared the three plates, I told Jocko about the encounter with the bear, the heroic actions of the elderly German shepherd, and the subsequent emergency vet visit.

Jocko enjoyed my storytelling so much that I kept going, telling him the story about my neighbor’s problem with the rat, and how it was that Adrian came to be the owner of a three-legged pet rat named Munchies.

Jocko roared with laughter the whole time.

After our dinner, we stood outside the restaurant, chatting under an awning while the rain came down. Neither of us wanted the evening to end. I could see why Josie had her issues with him, yet I could also see what was right with him. He worked hard, he cared about his craft, and he did seem to be interested in other people. Maybe not as much as he was interested in himself, but he wasn’t unforgivably self-interested.

While we were chatting under the awning, my phone alerted me to a message we’d both been waiting for.

“It’s Garnet,” I said to Jocko.

The older actor sucked in air between his teeth. “And?”

"It's good news. He said you can come to the house and introduce yourself."

"Really? Just like that?"

"Yes. He says his dad and sister are there."

Jocko rubbed his jaw. "His father is the one that flew down to LA to punch my other son, isn't he?"

"That's Dale Langtree," I said. "Don't be too scared. He hardly ever punches people, from what I've heard."

Jocko lifted his famous chin. "I suppose he owes me a solid punch, at the very least, for what I did. Jade told me they were finished, but I should have known better than to believe her. Deep down, I probably knew better. I made a mistake. What can I say? We all believe what we want to believe." He looked away, his expression relaxing. "Those were some wild days, at the Dragonfly Resort."

"I'm sure they were."

He turned to me, his green eyes wide. "We should all go there," he said excitedly. "I own the place. The whole resort. It's mine."

"Lucky you."

"Lucky for all of us. We should go. I can have it cleared out in a day. This is the off season, so at least one of the wings can be made private."

"Who is this *we* you're talking about? I'm not related to you or connected to you, aside from briefly dating one of your sons and working with the son you haven't met yet."

Jocko ignored my question and stared off at the distance again. "Actually, this week won't work for me. I'm shooting in Thailand. Just in time for monsoon season." He shook his head. "I need to fire my agent." He looked at me, his emerald eyes bright again. "Christmas," he said. "We'll have Christmas there. One big, happy family."

"We will?"

"I'll pay for everything, and I won't take no for an answer. Bring your delightful mother, Veronica."

"She'd like that," I said with a snort.

"Bring your whole family. Bring a few of your friends. And you can even bring that boyfriend, Andy or whatever his name is, if you're still bothering with him by then."

"That's a very generous offer," I said. "I appreciate it, but we usually keep things small at the Monroe home over Christmas."

"Not this year," he said grandly, puffing up his chest. "I insist that you do not keep it small. Tell Veronica I will be on my best behavior." He smirked. "As long as you don't leave me alone with her for more than fifteen minutes."

"Down, boy," I said, backing up. "You and I were having a nice time until you started making implications about my mother. Please don't ruin my good impression of you. My mother, cute as she is, happens to be very happily married to my father, Peter Monroe."

"Of course. I know that. You told me at least three times over dinner." Jocko let out another big laugh. "I shall bring someone of my own to keep my bed warm so that I am not tempted."

I snorted. "When you invite some lucky lady, please use those exact words. Let me know how it goes over with Ms. Bed Warmer."

He tipped up his nose. "Challenge accepted," he said.

The rain beyond the awning suddenly let up. There was only the dripping sound of water streaming off the awning onto the sidewalk.

I gave Jocko the address for the Langtree house.

He gave me a hopeful look, arms outstretched. "Hug?"

"Sure," I said, and gave him a hug goodbye.

"You're a good girl," he said. "I'll see you at Christmas."

"Maybe," I said.

He gave me a serious look. "I'll see you at Christmas," he repeated.

"Sure," I said. "Why not? My parents like free stuff."

Then he left to go meet his youngest—as far as we knew—son.

Chapter 20

I walked in the front door of the house I shared with Nisha. The house should have been empty, since Nisha was still at work.

Two men were on the sofa, throwing insults at each other while playing a video game on the TV.

"I must be in the wrong house," I said. "The house I live in—the one I pay fifty percent of the rent for—doesn't have any male roommates."

"Hey," Adrian said without taking his eyes off the screen.

"Hello," Noah said, taking his eyes off the screen to give me a courtesy glance.

Noah was Nisha's boyfriend, and had been for several months. They were not "in love," according to Nisha, but they did spend a lot of time together and had a respectful relationship. As for the "zoo noises" that Nisha claimed were constantly being made inside the house, the vast majority of them were made by Noah and Nisha in her bedroom.

Noah owned a yoga studio, and he looked exactly like a guy who owned a yoga studio. He had wavy brown shoulder-length hair, long, sinewy limbs, and a slow, deliberate way of moving and talking. He was utterly sincere in a way that got my hackles up, because I often interpreted his sincerity as smarminess. The line between utter sincerity and smarminess was a thin one—or at least it was to me, when it came to Noah. I hadn't forgiven him for all the years he'd spent toying with Nisha's emotions.

"You're home late," Adrian said.

The screen flashed, and he yelled, "Take that, Yoga Boy!"

Yoga Boy was Adrian's trash-talk nickname for Noah. Noah didn't use trash-talk nicknames.

Noah said to me earnestly, "We just started this round. We can start over if you want to join us. It's no problem. No problem at all. It is, after all, your place and your gaming system."

"Thanks, but no thanks," I said. "I would love to jump in there, but your fragile male egos couldn't take the pounding."

Adrian snorted and leaned toward Noah. "That's what she always says. Peaches is all bark, no bite. Half the time when she tries to play this game, she can't even figure out which character she's playing. She'll think she's winning because she's looking at your character. Meanwhile, her character is in a corner, bouncing its head on the wall repeatedly."

"Ha ha," I said. "That happened *one time*."

Adrian stage-whispered to Noah, "It happens *all the time*."

I went to the kitchen to get some water.

I came back out and said, "I can tell you're both dying to know why I'm getting home so late. The truth is, I'm late because someone took me out for dinner."

Adrian grunted and continued playing the game.

Noah grinned sheepishly at me and asked, "Who took you out to dinner?"

"An older man," I said, trying to make it sound as dramatic as possible.

Noah asked, "Was it Mr. Olivier?"

"Nope," I said. "Gordon's already gone back to Arizona for the winter."

The guys continued playing their game.

I casually said, "It was Jocko Ranger. The actor. We went to Niro's and had a very nice meal."

Adrian didn't even look up. "Sure you did," he said sarcastically. "Was your mom there, too?"

"No, but he does want to see her and catch up. He wants to see everyone, actually. He's invited all of us —the whole family—to stay at the Dragonfly Resort for Christmas."

Adrian's on-screen character crashed into some guard rails.

Noah paused the game.

Both guys turned to me.

Noah said to Adrian, "I think she's serious. I think she really did have dinner with Jocko Ranger."

Adrian said nothing.

Noah asked, "What's he like?"

"He's not a monster," I said. "He freely admits that he's a narcissist, but also that he's trying to be a better person."

"Hmm." Noah frowned and looked down guiltily.

I carried on. "He was perfectly nice to me over dinner. He's in town to catch up with his kids. All of them."

Noah's head jerked up. "That explains it," he said. "Was Garnet there at dinner? How about the others?" Noah was part of the inner circle that knew about my coworker Garnet's famous half-siblings and even more famous birth father.

I looked to Adrian for a reaction. His nostrils flared. The rest of his body was perfectly still.

"Garnet wasn't there at dinner," I said casually. "He wasn't ready to meet his father yet. They're actually meeting right now, at the Langtree house. His dad, Dale, and his sister, Perry, are there with them." I rubbed my chin. "I hope everything's going okay. I hope they don't have a giant war and ruin those nice walk-in closets that Adrian just installed."

"The closets will be fine," Adrian said through clenched teeth. "I'm sure the closets can withstand whatever is coming their way."

My mouth was suddenly dry. I sipped my water.

On the way home, I hadn't been looking forward to sharing the news about my dinner with Jocko.

The month before, Adrian had taken it poorly when I'd told him about my evening at the bookstore with the three half-siblings. Even though I was clearly with Adrian, officially and exclusively, he continued to be jealous of Dalton.

"How did it happen?" Noah asked. "Did Jocko Ranger just show up, out of the blue? Was it to see Garnet?"

I pointed at Noah. "Ten points for Noah. That's exactly what happened. But since Garnet wasn't ready to see him, the two of us went for dinner. I think Jocko wanted me to see that he was a good guy, so I could pass on a glowing recommendation to Garnet."

"But he's *not* a good guy," Adrian said.

Noah sucked in air between his teeth.

I replied, "If you're talking about the recordings of Jocko that went viral, with him saying all those awful things, all I can say is that everyone makes mistakes."

Adrian frowned and checked the watch and health tracker on his wrist. "It's eight-thirty. You were at dinner for over two hours?" He glanced up at me, his icy-blue eyes narrowed to thin slits.

"Not at all," I said. "Dinner was only forty-five minutes." I paused for dramatic effect. "Then I had sex with him in his limousine. That took a little longer."

Noah gave me a wide-eyed look. "What?"

I let out a chuckle. "Oh, Noah. You're so literal. Never change. It's really sweet."

Adrian said, "Two hours is a long dinner."

"Jocko's a great conversationalist," I said. "What are you accusing me of? Do you want to phone Niro's right now and ask the staff to confirm my whereabouts?"

"I'm not accusing you of anything," Adrian said. "Why do you always have to make everything as difficult as possible? I just said it was a long dinner."

Noah got up from the couch. "I'll just, uh, give you guys some privacy for a minute." He gave me an apologetic look before disappearing down the hallway.

"Now you've done it," I said to Adrian. "The children always suffer when Mommy and Daddy bicker." It was an ongoing joke of ours that Noah was our child who got upset whenever we argued.

"You started it," Adrian said. "All I did was comment on how long dinner was. You're the one who took it to sex in a limo." He turned off the TV, stood, and stretched. "But I suppose I did have that coming." He gave me a sweet smile. "You came home after a long day and found a couple of non-rent-paying moochers on your couch. That's not what anyone wants to see in their living room." His smile got even sweeter. Adrian could turn on the charm when it suited him.

"It's not so bad to find men on your couch," I said, also smiling. "One of them is really good looking."

Adrian waggled his eyebrows. "And the other one is your boyfriend," he said, moving closer to me.

"That's exactly right. The other one is my boyfriend."

He put his arms around me, leaned down, and sniffed my mouth.

I covered my mouth with my hand. "What are you doing?"

"I don't smell any wine," he said.

"Jocko doesn't drink every day," I said. "Just tequila, for special occasions. It's part of his... I don't know. He told me all about it, but it flew over my head. I think you could say it's part of his rehabilitation as a human being. He doesn't take drugs, not even caffeine, and he does a four-day fast once a month."

"Sounds like a monk," Adrian said. "Did he say they were monk vows?"

"Maybe." I shrugged. "So... are you still mad at me?"

"Why would I be mad at you for having dinner with a man old enough to be your grandfather? You think I'm threatened by Jocko Ranger?"

"He's in pretty good shape for his age," I said.

"He'd never be able to handle you, Peaches Monroe. You'd break him." Adrian reached down and squeezed my buttocks.

I gasped and pulled away. "Is that a crack about my weight?"

"Not at all. It's a crack about what an insatiable zoo animal you are." He caught me and squeezed me again. "Not everyone can handle so much woman."

"You're on thin ice, mister."

"That's the only place I like to be." He caught me and kissed my neck.

"Careful," I said. "Noah could come out of Nisha's room any minute now. We don't want him to see us doing the mommy-and-daddy dance in the hallway."

"Then we'd better go to your room," Adrian said.

"It's still early. Are you sure you want to do that already?"

"You had a two-hour dinner with a famous, wealthy man while I was sitting on your couch, playing video games with Noah. My dominance has been challenged. That means I have to take you into your bedroom and reassert my dominance."

"Your *what*? Your dominance? Are we role-playing right now? Is this a character you're doing?"

He slapped my bottom. "Get in your room now, young lady. You're about to find out."

Chapter 21

My father unfastened his seat belt and turned around to face me.

He and I were alone in the Monroe family minivan. It was early in the morning, and we were about to drive out to the Dragonfly Resort. The four of us—me, my dad, my mom, and Elliot—were traveling together. Adrian would be coming out in two days on the twenty-fourth.

Mr. Jocko Ranger was footing the bill for all of us to stay at the resort, meals included.

We would have already been on the road, singing along to our playlist, except both Elliot and my mother had decided to take one more washroom break before we set out.

My father said to me, "It's officially a typical Monroe road trip. We're thirty-five minutes behind schedule."

"Oh, Dad. It's a holiday. Nobody cares what time you get there."

He looked me dead in the eyes. "I have a massage booked for eleven o'clock. I am *not* missing that massage."

"Already? What about me? Do *I* have a massage booked for eleven o'clock?"

"How should I know? Did you call ahead and arrange one?"

"No. I didn't sign up for anything extra."

"You should have," he said. "There are all sorts of things you might enjoy. Various soaks, and skin treatments with mud and kelp."

I raised my eyebrows. "Is that what you're getting with your massage? A mud treatment?"

"Not until after lunch," he said. "At one o'clock, I will be getting a facial." He stuck one finger in the air. "Correction. I'm getting the *men's facial*."

"Is that a more manly version of the same facial they give women? How's it different? Is there a sawdust and beer in the mud? Are power tools involved?"

"No idea, but I'll take notes and let you know."

"Dad, I know Jocko Ranger told us to enjoy all the services available at the resort, but have you really thought this through? I hope you left some time for relaxing."

"I *will* be relaxing," he said. "I'll be relaxing through my massage, my spa luncheon, my men's facial, and then my men's pedicure."

"Jocko is a very wealthy man," I said. "If you're trying to get to him through his wallet, don't bother. You can book yourself for eight hours a day of treatments, like it's your job, and he's not even going to notice."

My father sniffed. "I've only booked three treatments per day. I'm not *ridiculous*."

"Of course you aren't," I said dryly.

"He's not *that* wealthy," Peter Monroe said. "Sure, he makes millions per movie, but that's gross. He has to pay a lot of taxes, plus the wages of all the people who work under him. Agents take a lot, too, and it's off the top."

"You may be right," I said. "Plus he pays alimony to all those ex-wives, and Josie's allowance."

"The daughter? I thought she was cut off."

"He put her back on again. That's probably why they're all getting along so well."

"Money changes things," my father said sagely. He stared through the van's window at the front door. We were parked at my house, which only had one bathroom, so my mother and Elliot were taking turns.

I leaned forward and squeezed my dad's forearm. "Thanks for agreeing to this," I said.

He gave me a knowing look. "You know I'd do anything to make your mother happy."

"That's not true," I said. "You've still got that dirty old recliner in the attic."

"Yes, but I installed a toilet up there. The bushes are safe."

"You did? But there's no room for a bathroom up there. A person can only stand up when they're in the middle."

"That's where I put the toilet," he said, beaming proudly. "No walls needed. Just a toilet, right in the middle. It fit perfectly over the stack for the main floor."

"You did not," I said.

"I did," he said. "Didn't your mother tell you?"

"She must have neglected to inform me of this very important home improvement. Probably because she's been so distracted by this Christmas vacation." I stared at him, frowning. "Really, Dad? You just put a toilet right in the middle of the attic?"

"It's at the far end," he said. "I put up a folding screen, for privacy."

"That's a relief," I said. "It would be a shame if your recliner had to watch you, unshielded, as you relieved yourself ten feet away."

My father tapped his finger to his temple. "I'm a problem solver."

"You are as brilliant as you are handsome," I said.

He beamed again.

"You're still very sweet to do this for Mom," I said. "I mean it."

He sighed. "We both know she was going to go regardless of how I felt. I'd like to continue being married to her, so I had no choice but to go along." He looked down and checked the temperature settings on the mini-cooler he had on the floor between the two front seats. In preparation for the two-hour drive, my parents had packed enough soda to supply a family of ten on a cross-country expedition.

"Besides," my father said softly, "it will be a wonderful experience for Elliot. A Christmas he won't forget."

"Give that kid some chocolate and a new toy, and he'd be happy in a train station," I said. "Actually, a train station might be preferable to a resort. He's way more into trains than he is into seaweed wraps."

"He'll have fun in the swimming pool. He's a water baby, just like you."

"He will have fun in the pool," I said. "Lucky kid. Hey, how come you and Mom never took me anywhere fancy for Christmas when I was seven?"

His eyes twinkled. "We've been through this, Peachy. You were our practice child, so that we could get everything perfect with Elliot."

"I knew it."

We grinned at each other.

Tentatively, he said, "I'm secure in my relationship with your mother. We did that whole wedding thing with the vows, as you may know. But how does Adrian feel about this vacation? You'll be around Dalton a lot. Adrian can't be too happy about that."

"If Dalton even shows up, he will be busy with his new family. I'll barely see him. He won't have time."

My father gave me a knowing look. "You and I both know he'll make the time, when it concerns you."

"Why are you bugging me about Dalton? I thought you and Mom and everyone else was Team Adrian."

He looked away. "I just want you to be happy."

"I am happy," I said. "I'm a naturally happy person. How do you like that? Your practice kid turned out great."

"If you say so," he said cryptically.

"What's that supposed to mean?"

The doors flew open, and Hurricane Elliot flung himself into my legs before scrambling over me to get to his spot.

My mother climbed into the front seat, saying, "Sorry, sorry, sorry!" She turned and gave me a serious look. "There was an incident. But don't worry. We found your plunger and took care of it."

"Oh," I said, then, "We have a plunger?"

She smiled, turned to my father, and said, "We are cleared for lift-off, Mr. Monroe."

My father started the engine of the minivan and began his pilot impression. "Folks, we'll be soaring at an altitude of ten thousand feet today. The weather is clear, and thanks to the tail wind, we should be setting down at the Dragonfly Resort by ten forty-seven, where the local weather is one degree warmer. Please return to your seats and ensure that your safety harness is engaged. Our friendly sky hostess will be by shortly to take your refreshment orders."

My mother turned and waved at us. "That's me," she said cheerily.

And we were off.

Chapter 22

Friday Morning

What a difference a day made.

On Thursday, my father had been smiles and chuckles, gleefully anticipating his spa treatments.

But now, a day later, the novelty had worn off.

He wasn't smiling or chuckling. He looked about ten years older, in spite of the men's facial and massage.

We were in the dining room of the Dragonfly Resort for the breakfast service.

My father had barely touched the food on his plate. He'd ordered his favorite special-occasion breakfast: pancakes with sausages and maple syrup. It looked incredible, yet he kept waving his fork over the steaming food and staring across the room.

Three of us were seated at a table set for four. Elliot was enjoying some screen time on his tablet, immersed in a game. My mother wasn't with us. She had excused herself shortly after ordering her breakfast, "for a minute," she'd claimed.

She was still across the room, perched on a chair she'd pulled up to the table where our gracious host, Jocko Ranger, was seated. Jocko was also at a table for four, accompanied by two young women who must have arrived in the middle of the night.

My mother was ignoring the young women, focusing only on the handsome action hero. She kept tipping her head back and laughing at everything Jocko said. I couldn't hear a word of it over the hustle and bustle of the crowded dining room, but I recognized the looks on their faces. They were flirting. In broad daylight. Before noon, even.

Since my father wasn't doing anything except stare, I waved at my mother and signaled that our food had arrived.

She looked right through me.

I put my hand around my mouth and called out, "I know you can see me, Mom. Stop pretending you can't!"

My mother held her hand up to block me from her eyes.

"Real subtle," I called out. "Your eggs are getting cold."

My mother continued her conversation with Jocko, unperturbed.

I looked around my table. Not a single Monroe at our party of three was eating.

"Elliot," I said to the youngest Monroe. "Screen off, eyes down, fork up."

Elliot reluctantly set the tablet next to his plate, eyes still glued to it, and began stabbing blindly at his hash browns.

I turned to my father, who still hadn't touched his food.

I shook my head and said to him, "Dad, now is not the time to get back on your diet. Not when the food is this good and somebody else is paying for everything."

He grunted and continued staring across the room at the man who was both footing the bill and entertaining his wife.

After a minute, I said, "We can't let good food go to waste." I swapped my father's plate for mine. I'd ordered granola and yogurt, which I'd instantly regretted once the waiter had brought out everyone else's food. Even Elliot's kid's meal looked better than the smattering of toasted grains and white goop on my plate.

My father didn't notice the meal exchange. I waved my hand in front of his face.

"Eyes down and forks up," I said to him.

He began eating the granola, chewing thoughtfully on the raisins and nuts. He still hadn't noticed the swap. He kept staring at my mother and Jocko across the dining room. His eyes narrowed. It appeared he was trying to read lips—a skill he did not possess, as far as I knew.

I dug into the meal in front of me, starting with the pancakes.

After a moment, I said innocently, "That meal of yours looks good, Dad. I'm surprised you went with granola today, out of everything on the menu. Why have something cold when you could have something hot?"

He continued to chew and watch Jocko flirting with my mother. There was more laughter. The expression on Peter Monroe's face turned from strong interest to deep disapproval.

"You really should have gotten the pancakes," I said, digging deeper into his meal.

The waiter came by to check on us.

I pointed down at the pancakes and sausages. "We'll need another one of these, if the kitchen's still open."

"Of course, ma'am," the waiter said. "The kitchen is open twenty-four hours."

"You're kidding," I said.

"It's true," the waiter said, smiling. "The kitchen is always open."

"And Mr. Ranger is paying for everything, all twenty-four hours?"

The waiter nodded.

"But not for room service," I said, shaking my head.

"Even room service," the waiter said, nodding his head.

"Wow. In that case, do you think I should pre-order my midnight snack now, or should I just call down at, oh, about eleven-thirty?"

"Call whenever you're hungry," the waiter said lightly. "Half an hour should be more than enough time, but do give the kitchen extra notice if you'd like something complicated."

"Is a grilled cheese sandwich with mayonnaise on top complicated?"

He smirked, but in a friendly way. "I believe that is well within the night chef's repertoire."

I gave him a double thumbs up.

The waiter refilled our coffee cups and our goblets of fresh-squeezed orange juice before leaving.

I leaned over and pinched my father on the upper arm. "Did you hear that, Dad? They have a night chef. I'm definitely getting room service tonight. Wait. No. I'm getting room service *every* night. And, when it's time to check out after Christmas, if you can't find me, just go back home without me. Don't look for me. Specifically, don't look for me in the closet. What's it called when you hide away in a hotel closet? Are you considered a stowaway, or is that only on moving vessels?"

My father finally realized I was talking to him and turned to me. "What's that about moving vessels, Peachy?"

"Nothing," I said. "How's your granola?"

He glanced down and grimaced. "Is that what I've been eating?" He looked over at my plate, then his plate, then mine again. "What happened here?"

Elliot, who'd taken a break from his game and had been watching us from his seat, laughed so hard that he sprayed my father's granola with bits of chewed hash brown.

"Dad, you're so gullible!" Elliot pointed and laughed. "Pee-Pee took your food, and you didn't know!"

My father tucked his chin down in faux indignation. "Gullible? There's a ten-dollar vocabulary word, Elliot. Where did you learn that?"

"At school," Elliot said, still laughing. "You're gullible." He looked at me. "Dad's gullible, Pee-Pee."

"Don't call me that," I said. "You're the one who smells like pee."

Elliot stopped laughing and gave me an indignant look. "I do not."

"Do too," I said.

"Do not."

"Do too."

My father suddenly pushed back his chair and stood.

Elliot and I both instinctively shut up. Now we'd done it.

But, rather than chastise us brats for quibbling, my father yelled across the room, "Veronica Monroe, your family is over here, and your children need discipline, and your breakfast is getting cold!"

Everyone in the dining room—about thirty people, between Jocko's guests and the other paying visitors, went quiet.

Jocko also pushed his chair back and stood. He spoke loudly toward my mother while announcing to the whole room, "Veronica Monroe, I do believe your husband has become restless!"

My father's face reddened. He yelled back, "Veronica Monroe, stop bothering the famous movie actor with your nonsense. I'm sure he'd rather be sharing breakfast with the two strumpets who were making a ruckus in his room all night!"

One of the young women at Jocko's table, a redhead, stood and yelled back at my father, "Who are you calling a strumpet?"

The other young woman, a brunette, stood and yelled at the room in general, "I am not a crumpet!" She then asked the redhead, "What's a crumpet?"

My mother helpfully said, "My husband called you a *strumpet*, dear, not a crumpet. Perhaps if either of you wore a shirt that covered more than twenty percent of your top half, you wouldn't fit the term so well."

Jocko turned to my mother and said, "Well put, Ms. Monroe, but I happen to enjoy my strumpets."

"As is your right," my mother said, tipping back her head to laugh again. "If I were you, I'd probably want a dozen."

Jocko waggled his eyebrows. "A dozen? Now you're talking. But that many girls would need a boss lady to keep them in line. Someone with more experience."

My mother covered her mouth and giggled, her cheeks turning red.

The brunette strumpet asked the redhead, "Should we be offended?"

The redhead shrugged, adjusted her tiny shirt, and sat back down.

"Oh, Jocko," my mother said, laughing once more. "You're such a bad boy. Try to behave yourself while I go spend some quality time with my beautiful family. Thank you so much for inviting us here. We are all having such a lovely time."

"I'm happy to hear that, Ms. Monroe." Jocko waved for her to go ahead. She did, and he watched her walk away. He specifically watched her butt.

I looked over at my father, whose face was redder than ever. He clenched his jaw to keep from saying whatever it was he was thinking.

My mother reached our table, sat down, put the napkin across her lap, and said coolly, "Eyes down and forks up."

Elliot whispered to me, "What's a strumpet?"

I began to answer. "Well, Elliot, it's a—"

My father cut me off. "It's like an English muffin," he said. "You toast it then serve it with butter and jam."

I said, "Dad, you're thinking of a cru...." I trailed off.

He shot me eye daggers.

It had been a long time since I'd lived under his roof, but I was still his daughter, and his eye daggers still worked on me.

Just then, the waiter returned with a fresh plate of pancakes, syrup, and sausages, which he set in front of my father.

"That looks so good," my mother said, inhaling deeply. "I wish I'd ordered that."

Without hesitation, my father said, "Have mine, dear," and handed her his plate in exchange for hers.

"Oh, I couldn't," my mother said, but she did, as she always did when he made gallant gestures.

We all resumed eating.

My mother caught my eye across the table and winked.

Chapter 23

Saturday (Christmas Eve)

Two days into our resort stay, I was already happy settling into a morning routine. I woke up when I felt like it—amazing— enjoyed a great breakfast—spectacular—then changed into my bathing suit to waste a few glorious hours poolside—heaven on earth.

That Saturday morning, I was relaxing in the hot tub while Elliot splashed around at the shallow end of the resort's indoor pool. He was playing with the only other child staying at the resort—a girl two years older than him. She was dragging him around like a puppy, and he was loving every minute of it.

The girl's mother, a brown-haired woman with a surgically sculpted face, sat on the edge of the hot tub, dangling her long legs in the hot water while she watched the children.

Snow was falling outside. We had a clear scene of the wintery landscape through the tall windows while we were cozy inside, enjoying near-tropical temperatures.

"This is how to do Christmas," the woman said. She spoke in a cultured way, like someone who came from Old Money or aspired to be mistaken for such.

"This is the only way to do it," I said in agreement.

We raised invisible wine glasses and mimed a toast. She held out one delicate pinkie as she toasted.

"Cheers," she said, then, "Did you know that Jocko Ranger is here? At the resort?"

"He does own the place," I said.

"I'm not certain if the rumors are true, but I overheard that several of the other guests are here on his invitation."

"Lucky for them," I said. I could have told her I was one of the guests, but then she would have tried to get more information out of me. I knew a gossip when I saw one. She must have only arrived the evening before. Anyone who'd been at breakfast the previous day would have witnessed my father facing off with Jocko over my mother, both of them practically beating their chests like gorillas.

"I'm Claire," the woman said, extending her hand.

"Claire," I repeated. "I've always loved that name. Claire, like the main character in a luscious time travel romance novel. Claire, who gets swept off her feet by a rugged hero from another era."

She blushed and fanned her face with one hand. "I may be a character, but my husband is no rugged hero," she said.

"Few are," I agreed. "I'm Peaches," I said.

We shook hands over the hot, bubbling water.

"Peaches?"

"Yes. It's a nickname for Petra, which never stuck."

"I can't think of a single book or movie with a Peaches in it, but the name is familiar. Isn't that odd? The only thing I can think of is..." She trailed off as her eyes widened. "You're that model! For underwear! The one with the big, round..." She looked down and squinted at my chest through the water.

"That's me," I said, bouncing them up briefly.

"You're thinner in real life."

"Um... thank you?"

She frowned at me and waved her finger back and forth like the arm on a metronome. "Wait a minute.

If you're *her*, that means you were the one dating Jocko's illegitimate son. That must mean you know the family."

I sighed. So much for me staying incognito. "I do know Jocko Ranger, but not well," I said.

She snorted. "What's there to know? I'm sure every layer is the same as the one on top." She licked her lips, leaned forward, and whispered, "Though I wouldn't mind peeling that onion, if you know what I mean."

"Get in line," I said.

She pointed at me. "You?"

I laughed loudly. "No, thank you. He's all yours. If you can get him away from his entourage."

Claire shrugged. "I don't mind sharing."

"What would your husband think of that?"

"He's my ex-husband," she said. "I'm free to do whatever I want." She waggled her eyebrows. "Or whomever." She looked over at the pool and yelled, "Rachel, no running on the tiles!" The she turned back to me. "How about you? Are you here with the younger one, Dalton Deangelo? I saw him checking in at the front desk just now, when I was on my way here."

My heart skipped a beat.

Dalton was there? The last I'd heard, he wasn't sure if he'd be able to make it.

Claire pointed at me and gave me a knowing look. "Don't try to fib your way out of it. Now that I think about it, I saw both of you at the check-in desk. Dalton and a voluptuous blond woman. That was you." She tilted her head to the side. "How did you manage to get changed and into the hot tub ahead of me? Were you wearing your bathing suit under your clothes?"

"No," I said. "Not this morning. I have definitely worn my bathing suit under my clothes a few times when I ran out of clean underwear, but not today. I assure you I wasn't the one checking in with Dalton Deangelo."

Claire smirked. "Are you sure about that?"

"He and I are just friends now," I said. "I'm with someone else. His name is Adrian. He's tall and blond, like..." I glanced over at Elliot.

The woman followed my gaze. "I see. I can tell already that your son is going to be a future heartbreaker. My little Rachel is only nine, and she's smitten, as you can see. Just looking at the boy, I can tell that your Adrian fellow must be very handsome."

"Oh, Elliot isn't ours," I said quickly. "He's my little brother."

She cocked one eyebrow. "Little brother? That's quite the age difference between you two. Your parents must have been surprised."

I nodded. "My parents were definitely surprised," I said, which was true. Nothing surprises parents quite like their teenage daughter unexpectedly giving birth in the bathtub.

She said, "It's nice that your parents have you to help raise such an energetic young man." She looked around. Besides us and the children, the only other person in the pool area was an old man. He was napping on a teak recliner.

Satisfied that no one would overhear us, Claire slid into the hot tub all the way. She got close enough to touch my shoulder with hers as she said, "Rachel is actually my granddaughter. My son and his girlfriend aren't exactly the responsible type. She's actually the reason my husband and I broke up. He wanted to travel the world, but I wanted to give motherhood another shot." She glanced down at the water, hiding her eyes. "Now that I'm older, I hope that I can do the job without making the same mistakes."

I asked, "Does Rachel know she's your granddaughter?"

Claire took a while to answer. "She's only nine, but she's very smart. She figured it out herself. She did live with my son and his girlfriend until she was four, so she has some memories. She's proud of the fact she has two mothers."

I looked over at the children, who were splashing around with diving flippers on their feet.

"She seems like a great kid," I said.

"Sometimes we get lucky," Claire said wistfully.

"You're one classy dame," I said in a fun, old-timey voice.

Claire said, "Maybe you could watch Rachel for a while so I can get lucky with Jocko."

"I take back my compliment," I joked.

Claire rolled her eyes. "Peaches, when you get a few years older, you'll realize the true value of time, and the value of going after what you want."

My phone, which was next to the hot tub, buzzed. It was a call, not a text, and it was from Adrian. I dried off my hands with my towel and pressed the screen to pick up the call. "You're on speaker phone," I said.

Adrian replied, "Why?"

I rolled my eyes at Claire and replied to him, "So that everyone in the hot tub with me can hear our conversation, Adrian."

There was a pause, then, "What?"

"You're on speaker phone because my hair is wet and I don't want to electrocute myself."

"You can't electrocute yourself with a cell phone," he said.

"Why not? If they can spontaneously explode, we don't know what they can do."

Adrian groaned. "Is your father there? Peter, is there any chance of a person electrocuting themselves in a hot tub with a cell phone?"

"He's not here," I said.

Claire decided to jump into the conversation. "Your wife is a very smart woman. She's just being careful."

Adrian replied, "She's not my wife. Who are you?"

Claire grinned at me and spoke loudly, holding her head over the phone, "I'm the hot tub inspector. Just checking the PH levels. Come down to the pool area, why don't you?"

"I'm not there at the resort," he said.

"Adrian!" I clenched my fists under the bubbling water surface. "You said you'd be here by breakfast."

He replied impatiently, "Can you just pick up the phone already?"

"No. Whatever lame excuse you have for abandoning me at Christmas, you can say it in front of... the hot tub inspector."

There was a long pause, then he answered hollowly, "Something important came up. We had to take my mother to the hospital."

I grabbed the phone and held it to my ear, no longer worried about the water.

"That's terrible," I said. "Is she all right?"

"Of course not," he said with an angry snort. "She's at the hospital, Peaches."

I didn't like his tone, but this was not the time nor place to address it.

I took a breath and asked, "What's going on?"

"She's knocked out for now," he said. "They're running some tests. She was at a party with friends, and she just collapsed."

"I'm so sorry. I'll tell my parents right away, and we'll drive back tonight."

"No," he said quickly. "Don't do that. In fact, don't tell them at all."

"They'll want to know," I said. "We're family."

"Fine. Tell them. But don't pack up or anything. My mother would hate to ruin your holidays. Besides, I'm sure she's fine. She probably just had too much eggnog."

"That sounds more like my mother than yours," I said.

Adrian chuckled. I smiled at the sound of it. He could be a grumpy bear, but it was worth putting up with his moods to hear him laugh.

"I should go check on my dad," Adrian said. "And see if the doctors have any news."

"Keep me posted," I said, and we exchanged goodbyes.

I dried off the phone and set it next to my towel.

Claire said, "I hope your boyfriend's mother is okay. I'm sorry that your Christmas isn't working out the way you had planned."

I shrugged and decided to make a joke to lighten the mood. "Claire, I will look after your little girl sometime if you'd like to get... an autograph from Jocko. Just because I won't be getting lucky this Christmas doesn't mean you shouldn't."

Claire's eyes sparkled.

She winked at me then extracted her long, very-fit-for-a-grandmother body from the steaming hot tub and went over to play with the kids in the pool.

Chapter 24

After our pool time, I walked Elliot back to my parents' room, which was a spacious suite twice the size of my room. Elliot ran in and leaped on the nearest bed.

My mother lingered in the doorway and asked, "What are your plans for the day?"

"I'm not sure. It's still a few hours until lunch, and unlike my father, I don't have a trio of spa treatments booked, so I don't know. I could take a wander around outside, or maybe I'll have a nap."

"You could do both," she said. "I hear the trails are really nice. The best one is about two miles long. You could take Elliot with you and wear off some of his energy. You brought your winter boots, didn't you?"

I backed away two steps. "Easy now. This is supposed to be a vacation."

Someone was coming down the hallway. My mother glanced over. Disappointment registered on her face.

"I thought that might be Adrian," she said quietly to me as the stranger passed. "Shouldn't he be here by now?"

"Slight change of plans," I said carefully, already feeling bad about the prospect of lying by omission. "Something came up," I said vaguely.

"Boo." She pouted. "Adrian is such a treat. I was looking forward to seeing him out here. We were supposed to play tile rummy. Is he busy with one of his business enterprises?"

"Adrian's mother is sick," I said, the words gushing out. "She's at the hospital now. Adrian told me not to tell you. I'm sure it's nothing."

"Oh, no!" Her hands twitched. "I'll start packing up."

"Don't. Adrian wants us to stay here, as planned. Astrid would hate to ruin our holiday. She'd feel bad. Adrian said he'd call soon with a report. I'll let you know."

Behind her, inside the suite, Elliot cranked the television up to full blast.

My mother rolled her eyes. "They shouldn't allow children in these places."

I laughed. "What would you and Dad have done? Left him at a dog kennel?"

"You *loved* staying at the dog kennel," she said, grinning. My parents had once left me for a few nights with a family friend who ran a dog kennel. The woman had put me in a large kennel and sent my parents photos for a laugh. It had become an ongoing family joke.

"I'm off to take my nap," I said. "See you at lunch."

We air-kissed goodbye, which we'd been doing since arriving at the resort.

I walked down the hall to my own room, which was a few doors away.

I was digging around in my beach tote bag for the room card when I heard someone else in the hall behind me. I didn't think much of it until the person had their hands on my buttocks.

My immediate thought was that Adrian had shown up after all. His whole story about his mother being sick must have been a ruse, a prank, to throw me off the fact that he was on his way to the resort after all.

Without turning around, I growled, "Can't keep your hands off the produce, huh?"

The person got an even better grip. "Evidently, I can not."

That wasn't Adrian's voice. I whipped around.

It was Dalton Deangelo.

He seemed as startled to see me as I was to see him.

The young Hollywood star let out a stifled, choking sound as he jumped back, hands raised. "Peaches? Is that you?" He was wearing dark sunglasses, so I couldn't see his eyes. Just his gorgeous, perfect face.

"You tell me," I said, chin lifted. "Exactly how dark are those sunglasses? Dark enough that you'd have to rely on your other senses? Tell me, when you grabbed my derriere like it was a pair of honeydew melons at a discount grocery store, did anything about that feel familiar?"

He grinned and pulled down the sunglasses. His beautiful eyes had dark circles, but they were as emerald and captivating as ever.

"I honestly thought you were someone else," he said.

"Who?"

"I, uh, thought you were the young woman I'm currently traveling with."

I gasped and held my hand to my chest. "I'm deeply offended. This is a million-dollar butt. There's no other butt in the world quite like it. At least that's what my agent would say, if I had an agent."

"Truer words have never been spoken," he said with mock seriousness. "I should have known better than to mistake your million-dollar butt for someone else's. Please forgive me for my mistake. In my defense, I am quite tired." He gulped. "And hungover." He looked down at his shoes. "It took a lot of schedule shifting for me to make it here in time for the holidays."

"Your story checks out just enough for me to forgive you," I said. "I'm glad you made it."

His eyes darted up. "You're happy to see me?"

"Not for myself," I said. "I'm glad you made it because your new half-brother will be so happy. Garnet wouldn't stop talking about you last night after dinner. My mom and I tried to get away from him by going to the adults-only lounge, but he followed us in, and the staff thought he was adorable so they let him stay. Your kid brother got them to fire up the karaoke machine, and he was singing duets with your father. You should have seen them."

Dalton winced. "Sounds like I missed out."

"You haven't missed everything. It's not even officially Christmas Eve yet. I'm sure there will be plenty of eggnog-fueled shenanigans for you to get into. Or tequila. Jocko doesn't drink, unless it's tequila. He says it works with eggnog."

"Ew." Dalton wrinkled his nose.

"Don't knock it 'til you try it."

His gaze went down to my chest and stayed there.

I was wearing a towel around my swimsuit, which suddenly felt like nothing at all.

He kept staring, so I gave him a playful shove on the shoulder. "Friends don't eye-grope each other's peaches."

He looked up and waggled his thick black eyebrows. "They don't grab them in the hallway, either."

"Try to keep your vampire hands and your vampire eyes to yourself, Sir Drake Cheshire."

"Or what?"

I tossed my head nonchalantly. "Or I'll tell your dad."

He wrinkled his nose again. "He may be my father, but he's not my *dad*."

"Speaking of bloodlines, is it true they're writing a new part into One Vamp so Jocko can make a guest appearance this season?"

He frowned. "Where did you hear that?"

"I'm still in your fan club. They'll let anyone in there. So? Is it true?" I dug back into my bag for the room card.

He avoided answering my question as he swished his lips from side to side and squinted at my door. "Let me see your room." It wasn't a question.

I didn't move a muscle. Dalton Deangelo? In my private room? With me? And with my recently squeezed buttocks, which were barely clad in a wet swimsuit and a too-small towel?

"I need to compare your room to my room," he said, sounding extremely reasonable. "To make sure my father didn't give you a better one than mine."

A maid passed by with a stack of towels. She gave us a knowing look.

Dalton said, "Just a room check."

"Oh, well, in that case." I turned and opened the door with my card.

Dalton followed me in. He immediately went to the window and threw open the thick curtains.

I glanced around the room frantically. I hadn't been expecting a visitor, so I hadn't tidied up, and it showed. An hour earlier, I'd performed some personal grooming prior to heading to the pool. The used wax strips, embedded with yanked-out hairs, sat right out in the open, on the room's second bed.

Thinking fast, I whipped off my towel and tossed it over the mess.

Dalton turned to face me at the same time. His eyes widened. "Peaches, I, uh..."

He didn't know about the mess and wax strips on the bed. To him, I'd invited him into my room and then spontaneously performed a striptease.

"Surprise," I said, recovering smoothly. "This swimsuit I'm modeling is from the new line of cruisewear. This one is a sample. You get to see it before anyone else. And... now that you have seen it, I'll just put on something a little more appropriate." I grabbed the nearest article of clothing, a cardigan, and pulled it on. He stayed by the window, unmoving, jaw slightly dropped.

I grabbed a pair of jeans and started pulling them on. Not the easiest task when your legs are damp from your dripping swimsuit.

As I struggled, he watched me. My cheeks burned with embarrassment. I soldiered on.

He asked, "Need some help with that?"

I snorted. "Don't act like you have any experience whatsoever getting a girl's clothes back on."

"I'm a quick study," he said. "Especially if I enjoy the work."

With one last tug, I finally got the jeans over my swimsuit bottom and zipped up.

"There," I said. "Now you've seen what you came to see."

"I didn't mean to stare," he said, turning around. Oh, *now* he was turning around. Several minutes too late.

"Not that," I said. "I mean you've seen my room so you can compare. Is it better than yours?"

He turned around again slowly, looking around and tilting his head left and right. "This room is way better, because it's got you in it. Next to you, Peaches Monroe, none of the original artwork or luxuries in my room can compare."

His words hung in the air between us.

"Don't be so flirty," I said.

"I'm not. I'm just being honest."

"You're *just* being honest?" I stared at him. We'd last seen each other a couple months ago, in October, when he'd been in town to meet his younger half-brother. We'd gotten along fine, joking around with the rest of his family, and hadn't brought up the topic of our relationship or why I'd dumped him. I'd thought the whole thing was resolved, water under the bridge, but I was surprised to find that, to my heart, it felt like no time had passed. I said in an aggressive tone, "Why start now?"

He answered evenly and calmly. "Because I've learned my lesson about honesty, thanks to you." He reached for one of the bottles of sparkling water on the table by the window, cracked it open, and took a long drink, draining half of it.

He seemed different from the last time we'd spoken privately. Older. Maybe wiser.

He gave me a quick grin then tipped back the bottle and finished it.

"You're thirsty," I said.

He wiped his mouth with the back of my hand and gave me a smoldering hot look. "You have no idea," he growled.

My skin tingled all over. My temperature was rising. Any minute now, my wet bathing suit was going to start steaming through the cardigan.

There was a noise outside, in the hallway. Other guests passing by.

The sound distracted me from my soon-to-be-steaming swimsuit, and something occurred to me. Something that didn't add up. Something I would have noticed right away, if I hadn't let my guard down.

Speaking precisely, I said, "Dalton, you and the other Jocko Ranger offspring are staying in the other wing, right?"

"We are," he said.

"That wing is newer, with a different color of carpet and decor. When you came up behind me, you knew you were in a different wing, and that this wasn't your room. And, if you knew this wasn't your room, you knew that my juicy bottom was not the juicy bottom you were traveling with."

He didn't say anything.

"It was no accident," I said.

He grinned.

"You!" I tried to look angry but probably failed. "You and your acting skills. You almost got away with it, too."

He looked down at his shoes. "So much for being honest. I'll have to try harder from now on." Then he looked up again, his emerald eyes burning. He raised one hand. "Peaches Monroe, I give you my word that I'll never deceive you again."

I rolled my eyes. "I've heard that before. Your alter ego, Drake Cheshire, says it all the time, and he *never* means it."

He snorted lightly. "Like you're one to talk. You've got your secrets, too."

I gasped in indignation. "I do not!"

He gave me a serious look. "Elliot is your child, isn't he?"

I was taken aback by the sudden change of topic. The accusation had come out of nowhere.

I took a step back, hitting my legs on the bed and nearly falling onto it. "Who told you?"

He grinned. "You did. Just now."

I let out a streak of unladylike words and sounds. I'd fallen for the oldest trick in the book.

"Don't worry," he said in a soothing tone. "Your secret is safe with me. I only asked out of personal curiosity, since the question has been bugging me for a while."

"I don't understand. How did you even know to ask? What gave it away?"

"Actors are good at studying people. We notice details that other people miss. For example, you rarely call him your brother. You always use his name." He stared at me with intensity. "It's almost as if some part of you wants people to know the truth." His gaze further intensified. "I think you wanted me to know. You told me, with the words you didn't say." He pointed at me. "And that, my dear, is *acting*. The good kind that actors get awards for."

I didn't want to discuss Elliot any further. I had to change the subject. "I'm no actor, Dalton. I'm not like you."

"All humans are actors, to some degree."

"You think you know me so well, but you don't."

"Then how did I know you wouldn't mind it if I grabbed you in the hallway?"

I crossed my arms. "But I *did* mind."

"Really? If you minded so much, then why am I in your room right now?"

"You're in my room right now because you're a manipulative bastard."

He winced. "Ouch."

"You *are* a bastard, Dalton Deangelo. If you don't like being called that, don't act like one."

He wriggled in discomfort. "I may be illegitimate, but my parents were married, so *technically* I'm not a bastard."

"You know what I mean. You're here with another girl, and you know I have a boyfriend, yet you grabbed me from behind and conned your way into my room. What do you think that makes you?"

He grinned. He was enjoying this.

I let out an exasperated sigh. "And what did you think was going to happen between us in here?"

He shrugged. "I figured we'd both have a good laugh. Would you believe me if I said I thought it would make a cute story?"

I shook my head. "Dalton Deangelo, I could have your career cancelled for something like that."

"Not me," he said. "I'm un-cancel-able, just like my famous father. No matter what trouble we get into, we only get more and more popular." He turned his head and gazed out the window at the view of the lake and the snow-covered trees. With a world-weary voice, he said, "Everything I touch turns to gold."

We were both quiet for a minute.

Then I held my hand up to my ear. "Do you hear that?"

He turned to me, his face in shadows, and gave me a dark, quizzical look. Gruffly, he said, "Hear what?"

"You don't hear that lovely music? It's the world's tiniest violin, playing a sad refrain for the poor little rich boy, the handsome Hollywood actor who can do no wrong," I said. "It's quite the tragedy."

Plainly, he said, "My life isn't perfect."

"But yours is a lot closer to perfect than mine," I said. "Now that you know I had a baby at sixteen, I think you're getting a feel for how much of a train wreck I am."

"You're not a train wreck," he said gently.

The compassion evident in his voice broke something fragile inside me.

I made an awkward sound, a choked-back sob. With my voice wavering, my lower lip trembling, I said, "If I'm not a train wreck, then why do I feel like one?"

He walked toward me, into the warm light of the lamp, and suddenly he had my hands in his. I'd been steaming a moment before, but now I was suddenly chilled. His hands were hot.

Looking deep into my eyes, he said, "What's wrong? What can I do to help?"

I managed to get the voice-wavering and lip-trembling under control. Barely. "My boyfriend isn't coming. I'm alone for Christmas."

He blinked once. "You're not alone," he said, then, "Why isn't he coming? Did you finally break up with what's-his-name? Alexander?"

"His name is Adrian, and no, we didn't break up. He had a family emergency." I tried to look away but couldn't. "I don't mind. Honestly. He has a good reason, and it's a long drive to get up here."

"I doubt that. I live in California, and I made it."

"Sure, but only because you had your butler fly you up here in a private plane."

He pulled my hands toward his chest. "If I were your boyfriend, I would walk barefoot through the snow rather than leave you alone for Christmas. Nothing would stop me from being here."

As I looked up into his eyes, I knew he was telling the truth.

"Dalton, I..."

"Shh," he said, and he leaned forward, bringing his face toward mine.

I should have pulled back but didn't.

His lips grazed my cheek. His breath was hot on my skin.

His mouth neared mine. I tilted up my face.

There was a knock on the door. A woman's voice called out, "Honey?"

"Shh," Dalton said in a whisper. "It's probably someone who forgot what room she's in."

The woman knocked again. "Dalton? One of the maids told me you went in here. What are you doing? Is this some sort of surprise? Did you get us a second room so we could put some distance between us and your father's bimbos?" There was more knocking. "Dalton? Are you okay in there?"

"It's her," I whispered, almost directly into Dalton's barely parted lips. "It's the woman whose buttocks allegedly resemble my own. It's my butt double."

Dalton pulled away and started toward the door. "Hang on, Harper!"

"Harper?" I followed him to the door. "Isn't that the name of the character in your movie? Oh! I get it. You're doing more of that method acting stuff. But why now? Are you shooting a sequel already?"

From the other side of the door, Harper said, "Who's in there with you?"

Dalton swung open the door.

Standing in the hallway was a voluptuous blonde, the same height as me. Her height and body shape weren't the only similarities. She had my hairstyle, my mouth, and my face shape. Her eyes were smaller than mine, but, other than that, we were doubles.

"Harper, meet Peaches," Dalton said.

Harper stepped into the room and came at me. I put out my hand. She didn't take it. My hand wasn't enough for her. She wanted more and she kept coming until she had her arms around me. She wanted... a hug.

Harper squealed into my ear, "It's so, so, so, so, so nice to finally meet you, Peaches!" She hugged me harder than anyone had ever hugged me. Like how a boa constrictor hugs its prey.

Chapter 25

Christmas Eve

Following my unplanned meeting with Dalton and his new squeeze in my room, I tried to keep a low profile at the resort. Despite this, I ran into Harper everywhere I went. She was in the gift shop, then getting a seaweed wrap next to me, then she was in the dining room in the late afternoon, swiping the last chocolate chip cookie right when I needed one.

When dinner time came, I met my family at their suite, and we all went for the evening meal. I managed to get down the hallway without running into Harper, only to see her as soon as we entered the dining room. She was already seated and waved cheerily when I walked in. She waved for us to join her and Dalton, or at least take the table next to them. I pretended not to have noticed.

My father liked sitting by the fireplace, but I steered everyone over to the least appealing table, by the kitchen door. That was the only way to put some distance between us and the Ranger clan. I hoped we could enjoy a quiet dinner together, just the four of us.

We weren't seated for five minutes before my mother turned into a social butterfly again. She flitted from our table to the others. She mostly flitted to wherever Jocko Ranger was.

My father didn't seem to mind, much to my surprise.

"Dad," I said at one point. "Can't you do something about your wife? She's embarrassing all of us."

He glanced over at my mother then back at me. "She's just having fun. Why be embarrassed? We all know it's not real."

"What do you mean it's not real? It looks real to me. What's gotten into you? Two days ago you were yelling across the dining room. Have all of your many spa treatments worked some sort of magic?"

He helped himself to another bite of my mother's untouched food. "It turns out I *like* getting cucumber slices on my eyes, and I like having time to do nothing but ponder the mysteries of life."

"Are you trying to tell me you have all the mysteries of life figured out? Including Mom?"

"I do." He smiled. "Jocko is the fantasy. The road not traveled." He touched his chest. "I'm reality." He let it sink in before continuing. "People can visit a fantasy, but they *live* in reality." He leaned in and said, "Jocko can flirt with your mother all he wants. The truth is, she's coming home with me."

I took it all in, and it clicked in my head. "Because you're reality and he's just fantasy," I said.

"Exactly."

There was cheering at the other end of the room. The Ranger clan was passing around the tequila. Dalton and Garnet's half-sister, Josie Ranger, was not partaking in the alcohol because of her addiction issues, but she was participating with shots of something else—olive oil. Garnet's other half-sister, Perry, and her boyfriend, a cute guy who worked in television, were celebrating the young man's recent promotion.

They did seem to be having a lot of fun. Far more fun than the other tables. Not that it was a competition, but... the Monroes were clearly losing.

My phone rang. It was Adrian.

I'd eaten as much of my dinner as I had an appetite for, so I excused myself from the table and ran off to my room for some privacy.

I closed the door, blocking out the sounds of Ranger family laughter, and fell back on the bed by the window.

"We can talk now," I said into my phone. "I'm in my room now."

Adrian replied, "Alone?"

"Yes," I said with annoyance. "I'm alone in my room, and I'm wearing a medieval chastity belt, as ordered."

There was silence on the other end of the line.

"Sorry," I said. "Bad time to joke around. How's your mom?"

"I've got good news and bad news. The bad news is I'm still not coming out to the resort, but the good news is she is feeling much better." He went on to give me a few more details about Astrid Stromquist's condition.

"I'm so glad to hear she's going to be okay," I said. Despite my relief over the good news, I was still annoyed about him asking if I was alone in my room, and it came through in my voice.

"You don't *sound* very glad," he replied, picking up on my mistake immediately, the way he always did.

I sensed the bait being dangled.

"Adrian Stromquist, are you trying to start a fight with me? On Christmas Eve?"

He replied sulkily, "Of course not."

"Good. We can have plenty of fights when I'm back in town."

He chuckled on his end of the call. My joke had eased the tension.

Adrian asked huskily, "What are you wearing?"

"None of your beeswax," I said. "It's nice to hear your voice, but I should get back to my family before my mother drains the resort's supply of tequila."

"Your mother's drinking tequila?"

"I shouldn't have mentioned it," I said quickly. "You know the motto. What happens at the Dragonfly Resort stays at the Dragonfly Resort."

"Hmm. Maybe I should drive out there. Someone should be keeping tabs on the Monroe women."

"Don't you dare abandon your mother when she needs you," I said. "I'm fine on my own. We'll be coming back the day after tomorrow. I promise not to get into too much trouble before then."

There was a pause, then, "Is *he* there?"

"Who?" Like I didn't know who. "Dalton? Yes, he showed up late this morning. With a date, or a girlfriend, or whatever she thinks she is. His father has two strumpets, so he had to bring one of his own. Like father, like son. You should see her. She's... unbelievable."

"Peaches," Adrian said with a note of accusation. "Are you being nice to the poor girl?"

"Nice to her? I can't get away from her! She's obsessed with me, Adrian. Every time I see her, she hugs me. She's hugged me three times today."

"She sounds nice. Good for Dalton."

"You won't believe who it is. It's Harper, the actress. She was in that *Waterfall* movie Dalton was shooting when I met him. They changed the script and let her go by her own first name in the movie. Apparently the female role was originally so two-dimensional that she didn't even have a name before Harper signed on. I guess they wrote Chubby Girl in the script for all her lines."

There was another long pause. I thought I'd lost him, but then he said, "How much of the tequila have you been drinking?"

"None," I said indignantly. "But I should be getting back to the festivities."

His voice thick and raspy, he asked, "Do you miss me?"

The sound of his voice wrapped around my spine and made my toes curl. "Yes," I said. "I sincerely wish you were here right now."

"That's my girl," he said. "Don't stay up too late tonight waiting for Santa Claus."

"Same to you," I said, and we ended the call.

I relaxed back on the bed and stared up the ceiling.

Something was stuck to my elbow.

It was the wax strips I'd covered with a towel earlier when Dalton had dropped in.

I got up, removed the hairy strips from myself once again, yanking out a few arm hairs in the process, then went off in search of my family.

In the short time I'd been gone, the scene in the dining room had gotten wildly out of control. Christmas carols were involved. My family wasn't in there, so I made a quick retreat before anyone saw me.

I found my mother in one of the cozy reading lounges, alone. She was reading on her tablet, sitting in a wingback chair next to an enormous fireplace finished with giant, smooth river stones.

I said, "No tequila for you? The party's still going strong in the dining room. I'm surprised you're not in there with them. They're singing."

She put down her tablet and looked up at me. "Good for them. Honestly, I'm feeling a bit worn out already, and you know your brother is going to be a handful tomorrow."

"Kids love Christmas."

"Your father said Adrian called. Is there any word about Astrid?"

"She's okay now," I said. "Apparently there was a mix-up with her heart pills and her thyroid medication, but she's fine now. They'll send her home from the hospital after a few more tests."

My mother let out a long sigh of relief. Funny how she hadn't seemed that worried about Mrs. Stromquist over dinner. Being in the same room as Jocko Ranger definitely put her in a different frame of mind.

"A mix-up with her pills," my mother said. "I guess we're all getting older. These things are bound to happen. Peachy, soon I'll be using one of those plastic pill organizers. I'll need reading glasses, and maybe a cane."

I took a seat in the wingback chair across from her. The wood fire crackled.

"A cane? Yeah, right. This from the woman who was smooching Jocko Ranger at dinner, in front of everyone, like the third member of his strumpet brigade."

Her cheeks reddened. "I wasn't kissing him, Peachy. *Someone* had to demonstrate the proper way to hold the lemon wedge between one's teeth as a courtesy to the friend taking the next tequila shot."

I raised an eyebrow. "Sure, but did you have to let him lick the salt off your cleavage? He could have used his own forearm."

"Oh, it was just a bit of harmless fun," she said. "Your father took a shot, too. Right after you left. He took it from the redhead's bosom."

"That doesn't make it any better. I hope Elliot was too busy shaking the fake presents under the Christmas tree to see what you two were getting up to."

She giggled.

I looked around. We were alone by the crackling fire. "Speaking of which, where are those two? Don't tell me Dad passed out already."

"He only had one shot," she said. "He's with Elliot in the kitchen, decorating a gingerbread house with the night chef." She reached for her phone. "Should I call Astrid? I should call." She made the call without waiting for a response from me, then reported, "Straight to voicemail." She wrinkled her nose. "Probably for the best, since I wouldn't know what to say. She's much friendlier with your father. I'll have him call her tomorrow."

"Sure," I said. "Or talk to her on New Year's Eve, when we're all at the party at their house."

My mother frowned. "Oh, dear. I hope the party isn't cancelled."

I laughed out loud. "Wow. You were really worried about Astrid's health, aren't you?"

She squirmed in her chair. "It's just that... parties are nice. When bad things happen and people can't see each other in person, the fabric of society falls apart. Nobody likes that."

"True." I settled into my wingback chair, resting my head so that it nestled in the crook between the wing and the back. "Ah. This is nice. Now I understand why these chairs have wings. Toss a blanket on me in a few minutes. It looks like I'll be sleeping right here tonight."

A male voice said, "I'm not sure they allow that."

I jerked my head up. The male voice was Dalton's. I hadn't stared at him too much at dinner, but I had noticed he was looking more rested and refreshed than when he'd arrived that morning.

"Dalton," my mother said warmly. "I was just thinking about how this will be quite the memorable Christmas for you. I enjoyed seeing how happy you were with your new little brother and sister at dinner. The three of you are adorable. A person would never guess that you didn't all grow up together. You and Garnet are the spitting image of your father. Such handsome boys. Jocko must be so full of pride."

"He's full of something," Dalton said. "Mind if I join you ladies?"

"Please do," my mother said.

Dalton looked at me. Some mischievous part of my brain mentally undressed him. I tried to shove the image aside.

"Whatever," I said, trying to sound nonchalant.

My brain undressed him again, faster this time.

I thought about how, just a few minutes ago, Adrian had warned me to stay out of trouble. I couldn't shake the feeling my boyfriend was watching me at that moment, watching how I reacted to Dalton's presence.

My mother said, "Pull up one of those chairs."

"They look heavy," he said.

She giggled. "Are those muscles just for show?"

"They are, Veronica," he said, grinning. "How did you guess?"

Rather than pull one of the other chairs up to the fireplace, he took a seat between the two of us Monroes, on the hearth. The seat was low, so his knees stuck up in a boyish way. His dark pants hiked up, revealing colorful striped socks. I couldn't remember seeing the man's socks before. I'd seen plenty of him, between our time at the Airstream trailer and our adventure in the woods, but I hadn't noticed his socks.

My brain mentally undressed him, except for the socks, which seemed much worse.

The three of us sat quietly.

Dalton broke the silence. "This is a real fire," he said. "It's hot."

My mother replied, "You're in the hot seat now."

"More than you know," he said, suddenly sounding weary. "I have a confession to make."

My mother started to stand. "I'll just leave you two—"

He stopped her with a hand on her knee.

"It concerns both of you," he said. "It's about your whole family."

I crossed my arms and waited. What sort of prank was he up to now? Was it more sophisticated than simply grabbing my bottom accidentally-on-purpose?

Dalton said, "Harper knows about Elliot." He looked at my mother, avoiding my eyes. "I'm sorry, Veronica, but Harper knows about Elliot's parents being Peaches and what's-his-name."

The words he was speaking gradually turned into meaning inside my brain. Harper knew. I'd only told Dalton my secret that day, and already Harper knew.

I had the sudden urge to toss a drink in his face. Luckily for him, I had nothing in my hands.

I gave him a furious look. "You told her? You couldn't even keep a secret for twenty-four hours?"

He gave me a sheepish look. "It's actually a funny story. You're going to laugh."

I crossed my arms even tighter. "Try me."

His brow was beaded with sweat. He really was in the hot seat. The fire blazed behind him.

Dalton swallowed, then said, "When we were all at dinner, Harper said something to me about a child's mother actually being their grandmother. It was noisy at the time. I didn't realize that she was talking about another guest—that woman, Claire. I couldn't hear her properly, thanks to the ruckus going on with the tequila shots, and, well"—he snuck a quick glance up at me before looking away—"I thought she meant *you* ladies and your family. Then I blathered something stupid about how surprised I was that Veronica told her about it, and that I'd assumed it was a Monroe family secret."

He stopped talking.

I looked at my mother. She was quietly chewing her lower lip, her expression hard to read.

I turned to Dalton, who was watching me cautiously through his thick, dark eyelashes.

Tentatively, Dalton said, "Peaches, is that the face you make right before you laugh?"

I looked back at my mother.

She stopped chewing her lip, gave me a puzzled look, and said, "Remind me again. Who the heck is Harper?"

Dalton started to answer, but I cut him off.

"That's my butt double," I said tersely. "When I'm not available, Harper is a close enough substitution."

Dalton sucked in air between his teeth.

I knew I was being unkind, but I doubled down and repeated, "She's my butt double."

"She's nobody's butt double," Dalton said calmly, not arguing with me but explaining to my mother. "Harper is an actor, like me. A talented one. In fact, she's far more talented than I am."

I snorted.

My mother blinked and asked me, "Is it true? About her talents?"

"Let's see," I said, beginning to count points on my fingers. "Harper has a nice butt, a hot date for Christmas, and she figured out our family secret in less than half a day. The girl has some talent, all right." I turned to Dalton. "Can she keep her mouth shut better than you?"

"Of course," he said, sounding relieved—like he thought the matter had been resolved. Sweat was now dripping down his temples. He shifted forward, to the edge of the hearth. "Does this mean we're good? All good?"

After a long pause, my mother said, "I'm sure you didn't mean anything by it. Dalton, you and I are, as you say, *all good.*"

They both looked at me.

I didn't have anything to say to Dalton. Or at least nothing I'd want my mother to hear. I'd opened up with him and talked about something I rarely discussed, and he'd betrayed me. Oh, how he had betrayed me. Starting the moment he had shown up at the resort with a busty blond *walking betrayal*.

My brain was no longer undressing Dalton Deangelo. It was imagining him tied up to railroad tracks.

"It's getting late," I said, rising from my chair.

"It's barely eight o'clock," my mother said.

I backed away from the fire. "I'm sure Elliot will have us all up early for presents in the morning, which means it's late enough. Besides, I promised someone I'd stay out of trouble."

Dalton didn't say anything. He did continue to look uncomfortable on his hot seat, which I enjoyed.

I gave my mother a goodnight kiss on the cheek, gave Dalton a goodnight glare, and left the room without another word.

Chapter 26

Christmas Day

At the crack of dawn on Christmas morning, my parents let Elliot into my room. He jumped on the extra bed until I got up. To say he was excited would have been an understatement.

He hassled me nonstop while I got up and dressed.

Then the two of us went to my parents' room, where we opened the presents we'd brought with us.

The whole thing was about as chaotic as you'd expect, thanks to the presence of an excited seven-year-old and copious amounts of chocolate.

Things settled down, and my mother got to work saving the fancy ribbons for next year. Elliot got busy with his new toys.

I was on my third coffee when my father pulled me aside for a chat in the most private place in the suite—the bathroom.

I sat on the edge of the tub.

He paced.

I said, "What's up, Dad?"

"It's time," he said.

"Oh." I knew what he was talking about immediately. He wasn't bothered by my mother and Jocko anymore, so he had to mean it was time to tell Elliot about everything. My mother must have told him about Dalton blabbing to Harper after I'd been tricked into blabbing to him.

My father continued to pace the bathroom. It was a really large bathroom.

"Elliot's having a great time here at the resort," my father said. "He's still so young, but he's a bright kid, and we figured why not get ahead of it before it comes out some other way? Your mother and I would like to tell him now, when he's so happy. This way it will be part of a positive memory."

"Cool," I said.

He stopped pacing and looked at me. "What part do you want to tell him?"

"Uh, none of it," I said.

"Why? Do you think we should wait?"

"No. It probably is the right time, but..." I looked around the room and tapped my fingers on the edge of the tub. "Your bathroom is twice the size of mine."

"Don't change the subject. Do you think we should wait? Your mother feels strongly that now is the right time."

"Mom's usually right about stuff. You should go for it, but without me."

He nodded. "That's up to you." He gave me a long, thoughtful look. "Do you want us to wait until you're ready?"

I got up from the edge of the tub and squeezed his shoulder. "You'd be waiting a long time. Go ahead and tell him today. He deserves to know. Plus it's a cool idea that it's part of Christmas Day, like an extra bonus present."

My father's shoulders slumped. "Or something for him to discuss with his therapist."

"Oh, Dad. Monroes don't go to therapists," I said. "We're too frugal. We deal with things the old-fashioned way. Suppression and alcohol."

He nodded.

I was overheating, sweating like Dalton had been the night before by the fireplace. I went to the sink and splashed cold water on my face. On the other side of the bathroom door, my mother and Elliot were arguing over how much chocolate was appropriate for pre-breakfast.

When I turned around again, my father was scratching his head. "What about Adrian?"

"What about him?"

My father gave me a serious, fatherly look, eyebrows raised. "He should be part of this. If not the telling, at least the deciding."

"What difference would it make if we asked for his input? We're three against one. We Monroes would outvote him anyway. Besides, I'm sure he'll be relieved that everything's out there so he can officially be proud of the kid. It must be a guy thing. You should have seen him that time a talent agent tried to scout Elliot at the park. He pushed out his chest so far, I thought he might break a rib." I waved a hand. "Go ahead with the plan. I'll give Adrian a heads-up. That's all he needs."

"Well, he's your boyfriend. You know him the best."

There was a knock on the door.

We opened it, and my mother slipped in and closed it behind her.

"It's time," she said softly. "I've just reloaded him with chocolate. We've got about an hour until he goes down for a nap."

"That's my cue to leave," I said, reaching for the door.

She moved to stop me, but my father explained to her what we'd discussed.

"Fair enough," she said evenly. To me, she said, "Elliot knows you love him, no matter what."

"I know," I said.

"Are you sure you don't want to stay?"

My father put his arm around my mother's shoulders and said to her, "Veronica, you know our daughter has her own sense of timing for things."

My mother bit back what was probably a sarcastic quip.

I gave them each a hug then let myself out of the bathroom, sticking to the suite's hallway wall so Elliot didn't see me, and made my escape.

The outer hallway was cool compared to the room.

I leaned back against the wall and caught my breath. I hadn't realized how hard I'd been breathing when I'd been talking to my parents. Why wouldn't I be anxious? It was a big day for all of us.

I used my hands to squeeze the tight muscles on the back of my neck. The muscles felt like stone. It was a shame all the resort's massage and spa services were unavailable for the day.

Now what? What trouble could I get myself into on Christmas morning, by myself, at a fancy resort?

I went back to my room, pulled on my winter jacket, and headed outside for a walk.

The air was crisp and refreshing. My breathing was easy, and my mind felt clear. The world around me was white with snow, and the sky above was blue and sunny. The temperature was hovering right around freezing.

I made my way down a snow-covered path to the start of the walking trail. It was a perfect day for a hike.

At last, some peace and quiet where I could catch up on my thinking. Like my father, perhaps I would discover the answers to the mysteries of life.

I had just cleared my mind of visions of a naked Dalton tied to a railroad track when I rounded a corner and saw a blond woman on a wooden bench. Harper. Alone. She jerked her head up when she heard me. I saw the unmistakable sight of tears brimming in her eyes.

"Merry Christmas," I said cheerily as I approached the bench.

Please don't try to talk to me, I thought.

She jumped up and ran to catch up with me.

"Mind if I join you?"

"It's a free country," I said, keeping up my speed so she couldn't hug me.

She kept pace by my side, saying nothing. She sniffed every minute or so, which said more than enough.

Despite how strongly I truly didn't want to know what she was crying about, I could feel my resolve cracking. We weren't sisters, and yet we were. When it came to eyes brimming with tears, all women were sisters.

Gently, I asked, "What's wrong?"

"Oh, Peaches," she gushed, and she seized me in her arms in a hug. With Harper latched onto me, I continued walking. I dragged her along for a few paces before I relented and stopped.

"Let me guess," I said. "Boy troubles?"

She sobbed on my shoulder then pulled back to stare at me, her aqua-blue eyes red from sorrow.

"I shouldn't have come here," she said. "He's in love with someone else."

"Dalton? Of course he is. He's an actor. He's in love with himself."

She shook her head. "It's another woman."

I groaned and rolled my eyes. "Not Jade again, I hope."

Harper took two steps back. "It's you," she said. "He's in love with you, Peaches."

I should have said something sympathetic, or reassured the poor girl that she was imagining things. Instead, I shrugged and said, "Can you blame him? I am, after all, spectacular." I'd meant it as a joke, but it came out sounding like I was stating the obvious. Which I was. But I hadn't meant it that way.

Harper let out an awkward laugh. "I'm being so stupid right now, aren't I?"

"A little," I said, relieved she'd taken it as a joke after all. "He's here with you, and you are, as much as this pains me to admit, also spectacular, but in a slightly more subtle way. I'm sure Dalton's feelings for you are real, and not an act."

She blinked at me. "Do you really mean it?"

"I'm sure his feelings are just as real for you as they ever were for me."

She pulled a tissue from her pocket and wiped her eyes. She was one of those fortunate girls who looked even prettier when she was crying. When I cried, it all came out of my nose. My mother and I were messy criers. I would have needed five tissues, not the one tiny tissue Harper was using to dab her pretty, red-rimmed eyes.

"It's hard when there's chemistry on the movie set," Harper said. "It can be so confusing. It's no wonder I'm so mixed up, considering that was how we met."

"Were you two hooking up while you were filming?" I waved a hand. "If that's too personal, you don't have to answer."

She shook her head. "I was seeing another guy at the time. Talk about a big mistake."

I remembered what I'd heard about them from Adrian. "Are you talking about Lars? Lars Lundin?"

She gave me a blank stare. "Did I already tell you about that and forget? I do babble a lot."

"You didn't tell me. I heard about it through my boyfriend, Adrian. He's cousins with Lars." I wrinkled my nose. "Really, Harper? Lars Lundin? He's kind of a dirtbag. He left a woman at the altar."

Harper shrugged. "I sure know how to pick 'em." She sniffed prettily. "Every relationship I have is doomed. I should probably break up with Dalton right now and get it over with."

A little too quickly, I said, "You should!"

She tilted her head.

"Kidding," I said with a swing of my fist. "Don't do that. You need to see where this thing is going. I don't know Dalton very well, but he's a decent guy... for an actor."

She smiled. "You're right! He is much better than most actors. Thanks so much for the talk. You totally stopped me from doing something stupid."

Flatly, I said, "Glad I could help."

She looked at the trail ahead of us. "Are we going to do this walk? It's about two miles to do the whole circuit to the waterfall and them back to the resort."

"Of course we're doing the walk," I said, scoffing. "Two miles is nothing."

"Then let's go," she said, linking her arm in mine and dragging me onward before I could think of a good excuse.

Chapter 27

For the first stretch of the walk with Harper, I silently stewed while she babbled.

I wasn't *that* fussy about how I spent Christmas day—I hadn't woken up with any specific plans, yet I wasn't thrilled about walking two miles with Dalton Deangelo's new girlfriend.

However, by the second mile, I'd warmed up—physically and emotionally. Harper was sweet. Naive but sweet.

Like me, she also had a story about not being allowed to ride a pony at a birthday party due to being overweight. In Harper's case, it had been her own birthday party, which made it much worse. I told her my own story, dragging it out slowly, and she made all sorts of excited noises as I did. She kept gasping and saying, "No way! And then what happened?" She made me feel like I was the most fascinating storyteller in existence.

I started to see Harper's appeal, besides her pretty face and great figure. Dalton was a lucky guy. He would be smart to hang on to this one.

By the time we got back to the resort, Harper and I were both giggling. We began play-fighting over who could get back to their room the fastest and safely use the washroom before wetting her pants from laughing too hard.

We got inside, and when we reached the fork in the hallways where we would part for our separate wings, we both paused. Something had changed between us. I'd actually become the girlfriend that she'd wanted me to be. And I didn't mind.

As we stood there in each other's company, all thoughts of our full bladders were shoved aside. Harper asked about my eyeliner, and we started talking about hair, makeup, and other important things.

The girl party was going strong when we were interrupted by Elliot, who must have heard me talking. He walked toward me slowly, his expression one of uncertainty.

I said to Harper, "I don't know if you two have been officially introduced, but this is Elliot Monroe."

"Not officially." Harper leaned down and offered her hand to Elliot.

He shook it and said nothing, which was unusual for the boy. Elliot was the definition of precocious.

Harper asked him, "Are you having fun here at the resort? Did Santa Claus manage to get all your presents redirected here?"

Elliot shook his head and gave her his grumpy face.

"Elliot," I said, a note of warning in my voice. "I saw the pile of presents in your room. Santa Claus got everything redirected just fine. Don't lie to Harper."

Elliot crossed his arms and glared at both of us.

I shrugged at Harper. "Sorry. Someone has had way too much chocolate this morning."

Harper started to say something, but Elliot interrupted, howling, "No!" Then he put his hands on my hip and shoved me. He was stronger than I expected. I stumbled back, bumping into the wall.

Harper said to him, "Elliot, that's no way to treat your sister."

He glared at her and yelled, "She's not my sister! She—had—me—in her..." He trailed off, glaring at my crotch area, as though trying to see exactly where he had come from. That was more or less the exact Elliot reaction I'd been hoping to avoid. "There," he finished, pointing at the specific location.

Harper looked away quickly. With her face down, she muttered, "I should be getting to my room." Without so much as a glance back at me, she hurried off, disappearing around a corner.

Elliot shoved me again, still glaring at my midsection.

"Stop it," I said. "I can see that you're upset right now, and we can talk about it, but shoving me is not —"

He shoved me a third time, and he didn't hold back.

I recovered, and then I did what any big sister would do. I gave him a shove back. It was exactly the sort of thing the parenting manuals tell you not to do, and I immediately saw why.

He went flying backward, landing on the floor. The hallway was carpeted with a thick pile, thankfully. He couldn't possibly have been hurt—not physically, anyway—yet he immediately went still and quiet in that way that makes every grownup's blood curdle. I heard his lungs wheeze as he sucked in air, and then the wailing started.

My parents must have heard it through the door to their room. Everyone in the resort must have heard it.

Veronica and Peter Monroe arrived on the scene to find their seven-year-old on the floor, wailing and writhing, face red, speech incoherent, and their daughter—twenty-something going on seven—standing over him, uttering something about getting a taste of one's own medicine.

My mother scooped up Elliot and took him away, cradled in her arms.

My father remained behind.

I said, "Aren't you going to ask what happened?"

He blinked at me.

"He started it," I said.

My father nodded. "And you finished it." It was such a Dad thing to say.

"I barely touched him," I said.

"It's okay," he said. "As you may have noticed, our great plan to tell him the news as a bonus Christmas present didn't go so well."

"I should have stayed for it," I said. "I'm sorry. I feel so bad. Why do I feel so sure about things when I'm doing them, but then still mess everything up? I thought I was a grownup, like you, but I'm not." I started toward their room. "I should apologize."

He caught me by the arm. "Just... give him some space for now."

"Space?"

I stared at my father. His expression was calm, and something else. Mildly amused.

He was calm and mildly amused? About Elliot's tantrum? I'd never seen that combination as a reaction to my behavior as a kid, and I'd never been the nightmare that Elliot could be. That kid could get away with murder.

I felt my stomach pulling into a knot.

My father repeated himself, still calm and mildly amused. "We all have to give him some space."

My words came rushing out. "He's seven, Dad," I said angrily. "Since when are you and Mom into *giving space*? I don't remember ever getting space when I was his age. You guys are way too easy on him. You're spoiling him. He's got no respect for me. It was cute when he was little, but it's not cute anymore. You need to get a handle on that kid before he's a teenager, or he's going to make your lives a living nightmare."

My father gave me a surprised look. "Where's this coming from?"

"Dad, he shoved me into a wall. That's not cute."

He blinked. "You seem fine," he said flatly.

"I'm not hurt physically, but I... have hurt feelings."

Calmly, he said, "In that case, I'm going to give you some of that space you didn't get enough of when you were seven."

Then he turned around and walked away.

Chapter 28

After my father walked away, I walked to my room on numb legs.

I took a few minutes to freshen up and put my thoughts in order.

Things with Elliot had taken a turn, but he was a resilient kid. He would bounce back. He would eventually stop staring at my stomach and lower. If he didn't, I'd make him.

We would work things out.

As for my father, what point was there in being upset that he'd become a better parent as he'd gotten older? As for Elliot getting spoiled, it was hard to say if that was actually true. Sometimes the distinction between well-adjusted and spoiled was a fine line.

Once I was feeling settled, I decided to spend some time in the resort's pool room.

I stepped into the warm, humid pool room. It was empty. The lights weren't even on.

I left the lights off as I slipped into the steaming hot tub. Outside, snow was falling. It was blissful.

I dried my hands and grabbed the paperback I'd brought with me.

I'd been reading for about an hour when I heard the door open. The lights flicked on.

"Oops," said a male voice. "The housekeeper said nobody else was in here." I heard the man walk straight to the hot tub.

I looked up from my book to find Dalton Deangelo standing above me.

My brain didn't have to mentally undress him, because he was already basically nude. He wore nothing but the smallest, tightest swimsuit I'd ever seen. No socks.

Dalton repeated himself. "The housekeeper said nobody was in here."

"She's not wrong," I said. "I would prefer to be a nobody right now, so maybe I'm radiating *nobody energy*. Have you heard of such a thing? It's a force field that makes you invisible. I like it."

"That doesn't sound like the Peaches I know," he said.

"It wouldn't, because you don't really know me." I leaned over and peered behind him. "Where's Harper? I don't know if she told you, but we're basically best friends now. I hope you don't mind." I tossed my book aside and waved a hand. "Ah, what do I care if you mind? You got yourself a good one with that girl, so you'll have to get comfortable sharing."

"I suppose I can share her with you, if that's how we're doing things now." He dipped his toes in the water. He had attractive, photogenic toes. They weren't too long or too hairy. They were just right.

He must have liked the temperature because he jumped into the hot tub. He actually jumped, splashing water all over me in the process and then laughing.

I wiped water from my eyes. "I should have expected that. You and hot tubs are always trouble."

He grinned. "Remember when we saw those deer?"

I snorted. "Remember when we ran half-naked through the woods while trained assassins chased after us?"

He didn't correct me that the assassins had been imaginary. He kept grinning and said, "I remember."

I turned my head and looked at the door to the change room.

"She's not coming," Dalton said, reading my mind. "Harper is taking a nap."

I raised an eyebrow. "You wore her out already, huh? Merry Christmas to you."

He looked away quickly.

I dried off my hands with my towel and reached for my book again, muttering, "It's a miracle this thing is still dry."

One of Dalton's feet rose up through the bubbling water in front of me. He pinched my book between his toes. Before I could stop him, he yanked the book down into the water.

I stared at him. How could a person intentionally submerge an innocent book? If it had been anyone but Dalton, I would have read the riot act, or placed them under a Citizen's Arrest. But it was Dalton. And so I just stared.

He hooted in delight. "Did you see that? I didn't think that would work!"

Flatly, I said, "Congratulations."

The wet book surfaced and bobbed between us.

He started a game of kicking it around the hot tub. I leaned back and watched.

He kept playing, kicking it higher and higher.

I shook my head. "Here we are at a fancy resort, with no end of entertainment options, and you're amusing yourself with a wet paperback."

He kicked the book high and caught it with one hand. His eyes twinkling, he said, "In life, we make our own entertainment."

"You can say that again."

He set the dripping mess aside on the tile and gave me a serious look. "What's wrong?"

"My parents told Elliot about where he came from, and now he's being a jerk to me."

"He's seven," Dalton said. "This can't be the first time he's been a jerk to you."

"It's different," I said. "He calls me names to get a rise out of me. I'm used to that. But now he *hates* me."

"Don't say that. I'm sure he doesn't hate you. Just laugh it off, like you do everything else."

Flatly, I said, "Thanks, Dr. Deangelo. I didn't know you were a therapist, too." I put my hands on my hips, though it was a worthless gesture, as he wouldn't be able to see my hands beneath the bubbling water. "And what's that supposed to mean? Laugh it off, like I *do everything else*?"

"I mean laugh it off like you do about everything *you* do. Not how you react to other people's mistakes, where you don't laugh, and you hold it against them forever and ever."

I stared at him. "Are you serious right now? I'm having a bad day, and you're making it about you?"

Slowly, he replied, "Not about me." He paused and pushed one hand back over his hair, squeezing the water out and slicking it back. "Well, maybe a little bit about me, but mostly about us."

"There is no *us*."

"Correct." He stretched his arms out and rested them on the tiles, affecting a relaxed pose with his body while his eyes continued to fix on me intensely. "And there's no us because you can't laugh at my mistakes the way you do at your own. It's kind of a double standard, don't you think?"

"Dalton, I'm over it. When you told me and my mom about your mistake last night, maybe I didn't have the best reaction in the moment, but I understood that it was an accident. I've already forgiven you."

He rubbed one eyebrow. "But what about my other crimes?"

"It's all water under the bridge," I said. "There was a time I thought you were only romancing me as research for your movie role, but now that you're dating Harper, it's pretty obvious to me and everyone else that you just have a type."

He blinked at me as another slow grin spread across his luscious lips. The hot tub started to feel smaller than it had been. We were seated across from each other, but the distance wasn't large. He was practically naked, within reach of my legs if not my arms. I could see every hair in his thick eyelashes, every speckle in his gorgeous green eyes.

His voice low, almost growling, he said, "I do seem to have a type, but Harper is just an imitation. You're the original."

I didn't say anything. I was all ears, no mouth. My self esteem had dropped after my childish fight with Elliot and then my father. Now my battered ego felt soothed by what Dalton was saying.

"Go on," I said.

He did.

"I couldn't sleep last night," he said. "I lay awake the whole time, thinking about how many steps it was from my door to yours. In my head, I walked those steps a thousand times just to knock on your door. I could see you opening the door, looking up at me, and..." He trailed off.

I tilted my head to the side. "Go on," I said again.

"You looked up at me, and there were various scenarios," he said. "You'd yell at me for disturbing your sleep, but then you'd invite me in. Or you'd slam the door in my face, but then you'd open it a minute later and invite me in. Or you'd open the door and throw yourself into my arms, then we'd fool around in the hallway for a bit, and then you'd invite me in."

"You have a vivid imagination."

"All actors do. How did you sleep last night? Were you restless? Did you think about how many steps away I was?"

"No," I said. "I had Christmas carols stuck in my head. I kept trying to figure out what figgy pudding was, and whether or not I would eat it."

"If you'd like, I can call the kitchen now and ask them to whip us up some figgy pudding. We could eat it together somewhere quiet and private." He raised an eyebrow. "More private than this hot tub."

I giggled. "I'm not sure I'd like figgy pudding. Some of those traditional foods have fallen out of fashion for a reason."

"If there's a caramel sauce, and I'm sure there is, we could figure out something."

I started to giggle again but stopped myself. "Bad boy." I waved one wet finger at him, throwing water droplets left and right. "You've got Harper, and I've got..." I trailed off, confused.

Dalton's expression turned to interest and then to delight. He bounced up and down excitedly, making tidal waves in the hot tub. "No way," he said. "What's-his-name is so forgettable that you can't even remember his name."

"Adrian," I said, relieved the name had finally come to me. "My brain is working a little slower right now because I've been soaking in this hot water for too long. Plus you confuse me, with your California-tanned skin, and your bumpy muscles, and your smoldering eyes. Look at yourself, Dalton. Don't you think it's a bit much?"

"Are you saying I'm too much for you?"

"That doesn't matter, as long as you're not too much for..." What was her name? "Harper."

"I don't want Harper," he said. "She's a sweet girl, but she's not you. I'm serious. Say the word and she's out of here. I'll pack her bag."

I pretended to be horrified, even though we both knew, on some level, that I was delighted at what I was hearing.

"But it's Christmas day," I said. "You'd kick her out in the snow, just like that? What would you do? Put her on a bus?"

"There are plenty of flights on Christmas day," he said. "It's actually a very busy travel day." He grinned. "What do you say?"

I pressed my lips together to keep from grinning. I should have been thinking about Adrian, but all I could imagine was sweet, naive Harper, crying prettily as she waited for her plane.

Dalton found my hand under the water and squeezed it in his. He looked deep into my eyes and murmured, "Just say the word. She brought a small suitcase. I'll have it packed in five minutes flat, and she'll be out the door in seven."

I kept my lips pressed together tightly as I shook my head.

He slid around on the bench so he was beside me instead of across from me.

Under the water, he took my hand and put it on his knee.

I didn't pull it away.

He slid my hand up his thigh slowly.

I didn't move an inch.

The hand kept moving.

My fingertips reached the edge of his swimsuit.

And then the door to the pool burst open.

Elliot and my father came bustling in, carrying an inflatable dinosaur pool toy that Elliot had received as a Christmas gift.

Dalton and I both shifted away from each other. We shifted in such a guilty hurry that we both went all the way around the round tub and ended up back together again. We bumped shoulders at the same moment my father looked across the room and saw us. He did a double take.

Elliot proceeded into the pool, fixated on his dinosaur.

"Peaches?" My father squinted then rubbed his eyes. "Is that you, or Harper?"

"It's me, Dad," I said. "I was just leaving." I headed for the hot tub's internal steps and climbed out quickly.

Dalton said, "Hey."

I turned around and looked down at him. "Don't stay in there too long," I said. "You'll turn into a prune."

"Think about what I said."

My father was listening, so I didn't ask Dalton to clarify what he meant.

Besides, I knew exactly what he meant. He wanted me to say the word so he could send Harper packing. He wanted the go-ahead to help himself to my bountiful treasures instead of those belonging to my butt double.

I should have told him to forget it, or that my answer was no, obviously, but all the excitement of the day plus the steamy hot water must have melted my brain because all I said was, "I'll think about it."

Chapter 29

December 26th

The Monroe clan left the resort early in the morning the day after Christmas. It was earlier than we'd planned to leave, but we all had reasons for wanting to leave early.

Mom wanted to get Elliot home again, where he could be in his familiar surroundings. She hoped that being in his own room, surrounded by his things, he would be reassured that his life was still as it should be.

Dad wanted to get back to his manly attic den and his garage workshop. He had experienced enough spa treatments to, as he put it, last the rest of his lifetime.

And I wanted to get away from Dalton Deangelo because I had been thinking about his offer. A lot. In spite of how sweet Harper was, I had been thinking about how many steps his room was from mine. I'd resisted him so far, but I didn't know if I'd be able to resist his smoldering charm if we found each other alone again.

All four Monroes piled into the van and prepared to leave.

Elliot wasn't talking to me yet, but at least he wasn't staring at my body angrily or shoving me. It was an improvement.

My mother settled into her seat and said, "It's a shame we have to rush out without any breakfast. It sure will be a long drive home with nothing to eat but a few granola bars." She looked over at my father and batted her eyelashes.

"You said we could leave early," he said.

"I said that last night, with a full stomach from dinner. You had to know I didn't mean it."

My father sighed and unbuckled his seat belt. "I'll see what the chef is willing to pack up for the road. Maybe something on a crumpet." He gave my mother a flirtatious look. "You know I like my crumpets."

She giggled.

Elliot, who'd been sullenly quiet until that point, yelled out, "Chicken nuggets!"

My father saluted him on his way out of the van. "Yes sir," he said.

Elliot began whining that he wanted to go with my father. I opened the door to let him out, and he raced after my father.

Once we were alone, my mother turned in her seat to face me.

She asked, "Are you and your father still fighting?"

"Not that I know of. Why? Did he say something?"

"Not exactly," she said. "What's your side of what happened yesterday?"

I took a moment to relish the experience of, for once, actually being asked for my own side. My mother's parenting skills had really leveled up.

I was too excited to speak coherently. "Elliot—he —he—the little jerk pushed me in the hallway, and then Dad took his side without even hearing my side. It was so unfair."

She blinked at me. "Is that all? I thought something serious had happened. I thought maybe the thing your father didn't want to discuss was that you'd slept with Dalton again."

"Did Dad say something about seeing us in the hot tub together?" Her expression told me he had. "We were just talking. That's all, I swear."

She gave me a knowing look. "I see someone has a guilty conscience. Tsk tsk. What would Adrian say?"

"Look who's talking! You're the one who was practically sitting on Jocko's knee last night at dinner."

"But that was right out in the open, in front of everyone. It was all a fantasy act, like being in a comedic play. We weren't canoodling in secrecy, in a steamy hot tub."

"I don't know what Dad thought he saw, but we were only talking."

She raised an eyebrow. "About what?"

I felt steam rising from my body. "If you must know, we were talking... about the possibility of... canoodling somewhere more private. Dad wasn't wrong. Something was going on, but it was just theoretical."

She said nothing. Her expression hadn't changed at all. She wasn't surprised.

"Mom, he promised me he would toss Harper out the door with a packed bag if I said the word. He told me she's just a substitute for the real thing."

She pressed her lips together. "The girl did seem a bit lacking in something. Sweet, though."

"So sweet," I said. "I get mad just thinking about him stringing her along. She deserves better, because all people deserve better. They deserve to be with someone who thinks the whole world of them, not someone who can take or leave them."

She frowned. "Who are these *people* you're referring to?"

I turned and looked out the window at the resort entrance. "I don't know. I feel mixed up, like how I felt the whole time I was in Los Angeles. Maybe I'm homesick. Being out here at the resort has been fun, but I'm ready to go home again. I'm actually excited to get to work tomorrow. It's only been a few days, but I feel like I haven't been to the bookstore in months."

She turned forward in her seat again. "It will be good for all of us to get back to our routine."

I asked, "How are you and Dad doing?"

"Fine," she said lightly.

"You can't be fine. This whole situation must have put some strain on you guys."

"Peachy, when a couple is a good match like we are, difficult times only bond us tighter. I love you children, but your father is my whole world. I'd be lost without him, and he knows it."

I muttered, "You don't have to brag about it."

"What's that?"

"Nothing."

I pulled out my phone and frowned at it. Adrian still hadn't replied to my last text message.

Chapter 30

Tuesday, December 27th

Bookworm Books was packed with shoppers looking for after-Christmas bargains when Adrian walked in the door. I hadn't seen him the day before, so this was our first time seeing each other since before Christmas.

I held my arms out for a hug. Then I saw the look on his face and dropped my arms to my sides. His expression was drawn, and his cheekbones looked sharp enough to grate parmesan.

He made his way over to me through the crowd and said in a hushed yet terse voice, "You didn't think I should be consulted at all?"

I had no idea what he was talking about. I looked around the bustling store. "About what? About the sale? It's not going to destroy our margins for the whole year. It's just a little promotion. And, besides, we always have a discount table for a few weeks after Christmas. Why should you care? You're not even my boss anymore. You haven't worked here in ages."

He grabbed my hand and pulled me over to a quiet nook. "I should have been consulted about telling Elliot," he said. "Your dad said something about me being outvoted three to one. Is that all I am? A single vote?"

"Oh, the whole thing with Elliot," I said. Despite telling my parents I'd give Adrian a heads-up, I had not. It was his fault for not replying to my messages. Well, mostly his fault. "Adrian, we would have gladly made you part of the discussion, if you'd been around. But you were the one who chose not to come out to the resort."

His pale eyes widened in disbelief. "Because my mother was very sick," he said.

I rolled my eyes. "That's not exactly the story Astrid has been telling. According to her, she was feeling a little woozy one day, and that was it. She says it wasn't even a big deal. She told my father that everyone else overreacted."

Adrian turned away and rubbed the bottom of his nose with the back of his hand. "In *hindsight*, I may have overreacted," he said without looking at me.

I replied, "Also *in hindsight*, I believe that you were looking for an excuse to ditch me for the holidays."

He whirled to face me, his pale-blue eyes narrowed. "*In hindsight*, maybe I didn't want to be trapped in the middle of nowhere with a bunch of phoney Hollywood types."

"In *hindsight*, maybe I shouldn't have invited you in the first place."

His eyes narrowed further. "In *hindsight*, maybe you shouldn't have gone, either."

I stopped the silly word game. "Why didn't you just say that to me in the first place? Since when did we stop telling each other how we really feel?"

"I don't know, Peaches. You tell me." His upper lip curled. "Did you have fun with Dalton?"

"I did," I said, and I began counting on my fingers. "We had fun in my private room, we had fun by the cozy fireplace, and we had fun in the hot tub. We had all sorts of fun."

His expression softened, as though something in what I'd said had taken the wind out of his sails, though I couldn't imagine what. In my head, I'd just started a massive fight. The fight to end all fights.

He slowly shook his head, his face still soft. "You do all these wacky things to drive me crazy, don't you?"

I shrugged. "Only about half of the wacky things I do are to drive you crazy. The rest is just practice, in case I get my own reality show someday."

He leaned down and kissed me. To my surprise, he didn't let up. It was more of a let's-start-something kiss than a nice-to-see-you-at-your-workplace kiss.

I finally pushed him away before it got too intense. "I'm working," I said. "There are customers in the store."

He herded me deeper into the corner. "It doesn't matter," he said. "The days between Christmas and the new year aren't like regular days. They're magical. All the rules are out the window." He tried to kiss me again.

I pulled my head away. "What are you talking about?"

"We are currently living in the forgettable days," he said. "It's all a blur. I could tear your clothes off right now, and nobody would bat an eyelash."

I caught a whiff of his breath. Alcohol. Adrian didn't drink much, let alone in the middle of the day. I waved my hand in front of my nose. "I think I know why this time of the year is a blur, at least for you. What have you been drinking? It's not even noon."

"Just a bit of mulled wine," he said. "It's a Stromquist family tradition to keep the good times flowing from Christmas until the big party on New Year's Eve." He looked down at my chest and used his fingertip to trace a line inside my blouse collar. It felt even more intimate than the kiss. "You're still coming to my parents' party, aren't you?"

"I wouldn't dream of missing it," I said.

"Good." He grinned and moved in closer. "I have a surprise for you."

I pushed him away and said sternly, "Adrian Stromquist, I know exactly what you have for me, and it's no surprise."

"It's something else," he said. "An actual surprise." He made a strange expression, like he was barely able to control himself from laughing.

"It had better not be a crate of rock-hard pears that turn mushy instead of ripe."

He rolled his eyes. "You're not still bitter about that, are you? It was nice of Gordon to get you anything at all."

"He knows I like cash," I said.

"The pears were delicious."

"They were not. You had to choke them down, and you did it to spite me."

"Did not." He grinned. "I promise the new surprise has nothing to do with pears."

"In that case, I can hardly wait," I said.

He jerked his head, pulled out his phone, and looked at the screen. "I have to go. I've got to hit the party at Luca's garage before the samosas are gone. Did you know Tina is pregnant?"

"Already?"

"Double pregnant," he said. "With twins. Luca is so proud."

"Wow. Things are changing."

He smiled. "They certainly are."

"About the Elliot thing," I said. "I'm sorry I didn't talk to you first. I really am."

He gazed at me softly. "I know," he said. "Some things don't have a right time." He waggled his eyebrows. "But some things do."

"What are you talking about?"

"You'll see." He kissed me again, then backed up, turned, and exited the store.

Chapter 31

Saturday Night

New Year's Eve

I finished wiping down the counter top at Bookworm Books. The store was empty and quiet. My coworker, Garnet, wanted to get to his own party early, so I'd traded shifts with him and was closing the bookstore myself.

The day had gone quickly. I'd spent a solid hour talking to a young woman named Riley, who'd brought in her resume. Riley had worked at another local bookstore—one that hadn't been as agile about survival as Bookworm Books. The girl had offered to come in and work with me a few days a week, for free, just so she could be around books. And so she'd be available in case a full-time job came up. I'd made a note on her resume and left it on the stack of paperwork for the owner, Gordon Olivier.

I turned off all the lights then stood by the door, reluctant to leave. I loved the store so much, more than ever in the new location, and especially when it was closed and everything was tidy. The books looked so peaceful, ready to sleep for the night and dream of their adventures.

I should have been excited to go on my own adventures. Tonight was the big party at the Stromquist house. Adrian had promised to reveal his "big surprise" there.

I wasn't exactly Sherlock Holmes, but I had a pretty good theory about what the surprise might be. Over the past few days, Adrian had dropped more than enough hints. The least subtle one was when he asked if my cousins who ran a flower shop gave family discounts.

He was going to propose.

Yay.

Why didn't that make me happy?

And why couldn't I find the energy to lock up and leave the dark, cozy bookstore?

I might have stayed there for hours except someone knocked on the glass door.

I turned to see my best friend and roommate, Nisha, standing on the sidewalk. Like me, she had also gotten changed into her party clothes at work.

I quickly set the alarm, exited, and locked up.

Nisha spoke to me with the exaggerated version of her English accent. "*Wot's* all this then?"

I kicked my heel to the side, striking a pose. "It's my party ensemble."

"Look at *the state of you*!" She shook her head. "That dress is so old. I remember you wearing that thing in high school."

"It's comfortable," I said. "For dancing, or whatever."

"For *whatever*? You must mean a visit to the tip."

"The what?" I knew that *tip* meant garbage dump, but I enjoyed playing dumb when she used English slang.

She let out an exasperated sigh. "You've got moth holes chewed out of the neck line."

"People pay good money for designer clothes with holes."

She was getting louder as she got more annoyed. "Peaches Monroe, that's not the dress you wear for New Year's Eve, let alone for the one with your boyfriend's proposal."

I lunged forward and clamped my hand over her mouth. Baker Street wasn't that busy after the shops had closed, but people were around.

"Shh," I said, keeping my volume low. "We don't know for sure that it's happening tonight. His big surprise might be something else. We've only been dating since the summer. It hasn't even been a year."

I was trying to convince myself as much as her. Deep down, I knew exactly what Adrian had planned. He could be unpredictable in small ways, but I was getting the hang of his mood swings, especially on the bigger stuff. Plus he kept dropping the biggest hints.

I released her mouth, but not before saying, "Your face looks different. There's less of it. What did you do?"

"I cut my hair again," she said. "I have bangs."

"That's it," I said. "Did your hairdresser do a blunt cut, or do I detect layers?"

"Don't try to change the subject. We're going home so you can change into something more appropriate for the occasion."

I gave her a suspicious look. "Are you in cahoots with Adrian? Did he tell you to make sure I was wearing something special for photos? Nisha, if you know, you have to tell me. Do you know for sure he's proposing tonight?"

She glanced around in a way that made my stomach lurch.

Then she said, "Noah has seen the ring."

The world started to spin around me.

Nisha grabbed my arm and held me stable. "Are you okay? Have you had anything to eat today besides half-sucked-on cough drops?"

"I'm fine," I said. "This is normal. This is just how girls feel when they find out their boyfriend is going to propose. You'll see when it happens to you." I gave her a questioning look. "You don't think Noah is going to drop to his knee for you, do you? Like a double proposal thing?"

She got a wistful look. "I wish. Maybe he'll ask in the summer."

I shook my arm free of her hand and took a step back. "Are you serious right now? I thought you two weren't like that. You told me you weren't even in love. You told me multiple times."

She shrugged. "Things change."

I started to shiver. The night air was chilly, and a breeze was coming through the moth holes in my dress.

Nisha said casually, "You know how it is. Love doesn't happen all at once. It grows."

I shivered harder. I didn't know what she meant. When it came to the important people in my life— my parents, Elliot, Nisha—I couldn't remember a time not loving them every bit as much as I currently did.

"We should get going," Nisha said. "Noah's already with Adrian, picking up some last-minute supplies for the party. Noah loaned me his car for the night, so I'm driving us."

"Darn," I said. "That means we definitely have time to stop by the house and get me changed into something that meets with your approval."

She laughed. "You are so weird."

Chapter 32

We got to our house, where Nisha went through my closet like a style assassin. She insisted I wear one of the new dresses I'd bought in LA. She handed me the fanciest one. It was silver and covered in glittery sequins.

I reluctantly yanked off the tag and pulled it on.

We climbed back into Noah's car, which was a nice Mercedes he'd gotten when his parents had upgraded his mother's car. Noah's parents were rich but not wildly rich. The Mercedes was twenty years old.

I gingerly fastened my seatbelt, careful not to ruffle the sequins the wrong way.

"I look like a figure skater," I said grumpily.

"You look dazzling," Nisha said. A minute later, she said, "Maybe too dazzling. I heard from Noah that the ring has a big diamond, but even a big diamond is pretty small compared to a dress." She started driving. "Oh, look at that. We're driving. It's too late now. I'm not turning around."

I turned on some music to avoid talking.

We got to the Stromquist house. The driveway was full of cars, as was the whole street. A number of people on the block must have been hosting parties. We parked on the next street over and walked up.

When we reached the driveway, I stopped in my tracks.

My feet wouldn't move.

Nisha gave me another exasperated look. "Now what?"

"This dress is wrong," I said. "I look like a disco ball."

Nisha's expression relaxed as her shoulders slumped. "You're right," she said.

"What? I do look like a disco ball? Wow. Some friend you are."

"Not that," she said. "Something's wrong, and it's not the dress."

I pointed my finger in the air and repeated her words as though I'd just thought of them myself. "Something's wrong, and it's not the dress."

My best friend nodded slowly. She looked cute with bangs. She waited for me to explain myself. She looked like a therapist in a movie, when the patient is on the verge of a breakthrough.

"Adrian can't propose to me tonight," I said. "Not in front of his family and my family. He can't do that to me. He can't ask me such a personal thing in front of everyone."

She played with her new bangs impatiently. "Yeah, right. That must be what's wrong. Because you're such a shy, private person."

We both let out a chuckle.

"It's wrong because it's too soon," I said. "What was he thinking?"

She said, "Noah told me there's a whole speech and everything."

I covered my face with my hands. "I can't," I said. "I just... can't."

When I dropped my hands from my face, Nisha was right in front of me. She put the keys for Noah's car into my hand.

I handed them back. "Thanks, but I don't think going home to change into a different dress before I come back here is going to solve anything."

She put the keys in my hand again. "Then don't come back."

"I can do that?" A moment passed, then I said, "I can do that."

She nodded. "I'll tell everyone you weren't feeling well. I'll make up something."

I grabbed Nisha's face with my hands and kissed her on the mouth. "I love you," I said.

"I know," she said.

"Have fun at the party."

"I don't have to go in there, you know," she said. "We could head home and eat those potato chips I've been hiding from you."

"What potato chips?"

"Exactly."

"No," I said. "Go to the party and have fun with Noah. It's New Year's Eve. Your first one together. I'm sure it will be memorable."

She grabbed my face in her hands and kissed me back. "Happy New Year," she said.

I started walking back down the hill toward the car, keeping my head down in case anyone I knew was on their way in.

When I got to the car, I realized that Adrian might come looking for me at the house. He'd probably insist on doing the proposal there, no matter how convincing my sick act was.

Where could I go that he couldn't find me?

I got in the vehicle and started driving.

I didn't know where I was going, but my foot on the gas and my hands on the wheel all seemed to have an idea.

When I reached the outskirts of the city, I realized where I was headed.

An hour out of the city, I pulled into a service station to get supplies for a long drive.

The attendant at the service station looked down at my sequined dress and said, "Someone's going somewhere fancy."

"I sure am," I said. "I'm driving to Los Angeles."

He whistled. "That's a long drive."
"That's why I'm wearing sequins."
Politely, he said, "That's a new one."

Chapter 33

I drove into the night.

Midnight passed without any fireworks, fanfare, or kissing.

I drove for miles and miles in the Mercedes that used to belong to Noah's mom.

I kept expecting to get the urge to turn around, but it wasn't happening. I felt more certain about this crazy road trip than I'd ever felt about, say, picking the right shade of lipstick.

The sun rose.

I kept driving. The Mercedes sailed down the highway like a dream.

I stopped only for car supplies, washroom breaks, and once to buy an adapter and charger for my phone.

Every time I stopped, the employees and other customers in the stores looked me over and gave me sly, knowing looks. It was early morning on New Year's Day, and I was very obviously dressed in the previous night's cocktail dress. They all thought they knew my story—that I'd spent the night at a stranger's house. Little did they know the truth was much more scandalous.

I wasn't just a sleep-deprived girl in last night's sequins. I was a girl who'd left her tall, blond boyfriend—and his engagement ring—to drive all night in a borrowed car—make that a *stolen* car—so I could "drop in" on a Hollywood bad-boy actor. An actor who couldn't possibly be good for me.

I returned their knowing stares with a cheerful wave and carried on.

The driving became more stressful as I neared Los Angeles with all its busy highways. I had a valid driver's license but no car, so I rarely drove, let alone through an unfamiliar urban sprawl like that around LA.

However, my trusty phone and its navigation didn't let me down.

Neither did my LA-based friend Mitchell. It was thanks to Mitchell and his business connections that I had an address for my final destination: Dalton Deangelo's residence in the Hollywood hills.

"You're the absolute best," I said to Mitchell over the speakerphone as I turned onto Dalton's street.

His squeaky voice came back to me, vibrating with excitement. "You bet your sweet peaches I'm the best. I'm your first, best, and only friend in this dirty ol' town. Welcome back, girl. I can't wait to see you!"

"Don't get too excited. I might be making a U-turn and heading right back home in ten minutes. Right after Dalton laughs in my face."

"He's not going to laugh in your face," Mitchell said. "It's going to be so romantic. I wish I could be there to see it. Good luck! Bye!"

"Wait! Maybe I should go over my speech with you one more time," I said.

"Kill me," Mitchell said with a groan. "If you start with that awful speech again, so help me, I'm hanging up."

"I'm not sure about some of the wording. I need to get it right, Mitchell."

"Why? Guys don't care about speeches. Trust me."

I sighed.

Suddenly, there was movement ahead of me. The secure entrance to Dalton's home—a solid gate—was opening. I had reached the fortified castle, and now the drawbridge was being let down.

Panicked, I said, "The gate's opening. Mitchell, why is the gate opening? I haven't even buzzed the house yet. Are you sure you gave me the right address?"

"If the gate's opening, maybe the butler saw your Mercedes and figured that was good enough." He muttered, "Must be nice to have a security gate. And a butler. I think my nosy landlady lets herself into my apartment when I'm not home. I keep finding fresh fruit in my fridge, and I don't remember buying it."

I didn't say anything about Mitchell's fruit/landlady issue. I was too focused on driving up the narrow driveway. Dalton Deangelo's driveway. In Hollywood!

Mitchell made a yawning sound and said, "I should probably get some sleep, or some more booze. Hmm. What to do, what to do? Booze it is. I'm hanging up now to go in search of crushed ice. Call me as soon as the romance settles down." He snickered. "You can let me know how good the reunion was, starting with how many times you reunited."

"We'll see about that. Thanks for everything," I said, and I promised to be in touch soon.

"Happy New Year," Mitchell said before the call ended.

I parked the car, stepped out, and paused. What was I forgetting? My hands were empty. I had nothing but the clothes on my back and a tiny purse. I had forgotten... everything. That's what I'd forgotten.

Too late now.

I headed toward what I guessed was the front door.

I rang the doorbell.

On the other side of the door, Dalton yelled to someone, "I'm right by the door, so I'll get it!"

The door opened.

There he was. Shirtless. Wearing a pair of gray sweatpants and nothing else. His dark hair was bed-tousled, and his face was sleepy. His emerald-green eyes widened as he saw it was me at the door. He did a double take that turned into a triple take.

I opened my mouth and managed to croak out a nervous greeting. "Oh, good. You're home."

His jaw dropped. He pushed it closed with his hand.

He started to say something, but I stopped him with a wave of my hand.

"Before you say a single word, there's something I want to tell you. Something I *need* to tell you."

He waved for me to step inside the house with him.

I held back. I'd been sitting for hours, and standing felt right. Standing was a good position from which to start running.

"If it's all the same, I'd rather do it right here," I said. "This is how I rehearsed it."

The handsome actor raised one dark, sexy eyebrow then leaned against the doorframe casually.

"Dalton, I've been thinking about what you said to me that day in the hot tub. How you made it clear the choice was up to me. You made it sound like I still had to make the choice, even though I'd already chosen, and made the right choice. The right choice is for me to be with Adrian. It's so obvious. He's Elliot's father, which makes him already part of the family, and everyone loves him. Plus I've known him forever. I've wanted to be with him since we were teenagers. I had such a raging crush on him, and he was my first lover. The two of us have great chemistry with each other. Like, amazing chemistry. Physically."

Dalton's brow furrowed. Mitchell had guessed Dalton wouldn't like that part of the speech.

"I'm only telling you about the chemistry because I want to be perfectly honest," I said. "Maybe that makes me a bad person, that I care about physical chemistry, but it is what it is. I'm a bad person. A bad girl who likes..." I trailed off, dismayed that I'd started improvising and lost my place in the speech. Where was I?

"The thing is," I said, struggling to find some of the words I'd gotten so carefully arranged in my head on the long overnight drive to LA.

"The thing is," I said again. "You aren't my dad."

Dalton gave me a sidelong, confused look.

"Oops. I mean Adrian isn't my dad," I said. "And you aren't Jocko Ranger. And I'm not my mother. Furthermore, my life isn't a copy of my mom's. Just because she made the right choice and married the boring, stable guy instead of the famous actor, that doesn't mean it's the right choice for me." I realized what I'd just said about marriage and waved a hand desperately. "Not that I'm saying I want to get married! Not to you! I mean, not right away!"

He gave me an amused smile.

"I'm very confused right now," I admitted. My speech was completely gone. "I'm confused, but I knew I had to come here, Dalton. I had to see you." I glanced over my shoulder at the Mercedes. The reality of what I'd done was starting to sink in. I turned back to Dalton and said softly, "I stole that car."

He stepped forward onto the concrete step.

I could feel the heat radiating from his bare chest onto my bare arms.

He leaned down and kissed me lightly.

When I didn't pull away, he put his arms around me and kissed me again, longer. I didn't want it to ever stop.

He finally pulled away and looked down into my eyes. Then he began to laugh, low and rumbling.

"What?" I asked. "What's going on? Why are you laughing at me? It was the speech, wasn't it? I knew I should have written some notes on my hand. Or simplified."

He shook his head, still smiling.

"I should have done better," I said. "Forget this happened. Let's yell cut and shoot another take. Go back into the house, and I'll ring the doorbell again."

He smiled down at me.

"What?" I blinked up at him. "Say something."

"You didn't need to give me a speech," he said.

"Great. Now I'll have to tell Mitchell he was right about everything."

"Who's Mitchell?" He gave his head a shake. "Never mind. I don't need to know. In any case, you didn't need notes, or a different speech, or any speech."

I stepped back. "Because you're sending me back home again?"

"Oh, Peaches," he said. "You didn't need a speech... because you had me at 'Oh, good. You're home.'"

"I did?"

He could have reassured me with his words that I did, indeed, have him, but then he did something better. He showed me with a kiss.

The California sunshine warmed the top of my head. Dalton's kiss warmed my whole body.

Birds chirped around us. The moment was both surreal and real at the same time. I felt like I was floating but also like I was more grounded than I'd ever been. In Dalton's arms.

And it was New Year's Day.

I didn't know what would happen next, but it was already the *newest* any new year had ever been.

Just then, Dalton's butler, Bernard, came to see what all the fuss at the front door was about. When he saw it was me, he squealed in a non-Bernard manner and hugged me even harder than Dalton had.

Dalton stepped back into the house, excusing himself to check on something inside.

Bernard murmured in my ear, "You got here just in time."

"I did?"

The refined butler pulled back and gave me an enigmatic look. "You have no idea," he said softly.

And so, the next part of *the newest of new years ever* began to unfold.

The end of Book 3, Everything is Peaches.

The story concludes in Book 4, Peaches on Top by Angie Pepper